P9-DTR-192

Livoni, Cathy, 1956-
    Element of time / Cathy Livoni. --
1st ed. -- San Diego : Harcourt Brace
Jovanovich, c1983.
    182 p. ; 22 cm.

    ISBN 0-15-225369-6 : $12.95

    I. Title.

ELEMENT OF TIME

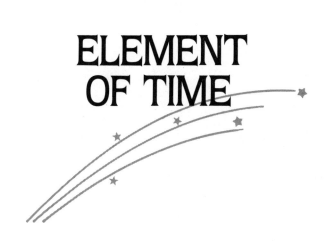

ELEMENT OF TIME

CATHY LIVONI

Harcourt Brace Jovanovich

San Diego New York London

Book Designer—Mark Likgalter

Printed in the United States of America

Library of Congress Cataloging in Publication Data

Livoni, Cathy, 1956-
    Element of time.

    Summary: Sael, a young man classed as unstable
because of his violent emotions and bizarre visions,
experiences a terrifyingly vivid premonition of the
destruction of his world by a powerful intergalactic
force.
    [1. Science fiction.   2. Extrasensory perception—
Fiction]   I. Title.
PZ7.L765El   1983   [Fic]   82-48761
ISBN 0-15-225369-6

B C D E   First edition

To

Penny Williams,
Trevor Meldal-Johnsen,
and especially my parents,
Ralph and Dorrie Livoni—

Thanks! It's about time!

ELEMENT OF TIME

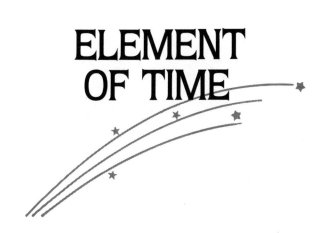

Chapter 1

THE LAVENDER-GRAY TWILIGHT OF a clear spring evening had fallen over the city of Lym when Sael glanced out the window of the academy classroom. His thoughts drifted from M'Goba's droning lecture on flight procedures, which Sael already knew, to the premonition he had received the night before: the sleek, unfamiliar ship; the fire unleashed upon the city; the churning mass of feelings. It had been so clear, yet he could not tell when it would happen! Sael shut it firmly out of his mind. The sense of reality was too strong, the impressions too horrible to visualize again.

"Sael!" M'Goba's command brought him back to the present. "Either keep your attention on this class or leave it entirely. I shouldn't need to remind you that once you leave, you will not be allowed back into the academy. You have been given more than enough chances here."

That ends everything right there, Sael thought. *I'll never make it to the space center if I drop out.* But who was he kidding? Here in the academy he had been juggled from class to class. Right now he was three classes behind where he ought to be, and Sael knew that the instructors had not given him the real reason for it. It was his unstable emotional nature, he thought. Something made his emotions unreliable, almost impossible to control. Whatever it was, it also occasionally gave him the power to see distant places and other times. However, he had no discipline over the power, no choice as to what it would show him, how much he could see with it, or when it would work. Sometimes he got entire scenes; other times only a vague flash of a place he had never been to or a time in the future.

"Do I have your answer?" said the instructor.

Involuntary tears stung Sael's eyes, and he rose, his decision made. "I cannot keep your class, M'Goba."

The instructor nodded stiffly and turned away. As Sael left the room with his belongings under his arm, the eyes of the other students avoided him, but he sensed their thoughts.

He was free, he thought, walking the long eastern corridor of the academy, but not happy, and he wondered what he should do now. Go back into internal technology? Well, it was an option. Even though he didn't like it, at least it paid well.

Sael came to the end of the corridor and stopped in front of the blue glass doors leading into the space center. It had been eleven days since he'd been in there. The orange student band on his left arm allowed him into most areas of the center, and since he still had authorization...

Entering the familiar complex, Sael walked slowly along the corridors. Glistening walls arched to silver-blue ceilings, and broad polished buttresses curiously distorted the reflection of his tall, lean frame. The long-sleeved light-green jump suit he wore was bound snugly about his waist with a technician's utility belt. His dust-blond hair was thick and wavy, and while the styling softened his angular features and high cheekbones, the color was almost too light to complement his deep reddish-bronze skin.

The faint sound of his boots against the resilient flax-metal floor echoed rhythmically with the distant hums, sibilant sighs, and sudden silences coming from deep within the great complex. It was alive, he thought, pulsating, steadily pouring vital energies through its myriad of rooms and inner chambers, even to this very corridor.

Most people had left for the day. Sael walked through the empty corridors, too engrossed in anxiety about the premonition to notice that he was winding deeper and deeper into the heart of the complex. Then a movement down the hall caught his eye. He came to a shocked halt and stared at the two silver-clad men who were heading toward him. They appeared to be in deep mental communication with each other and unaware of him.

Councilmen! Sael recognized one as the aging First Councillor Hedrick, and the other as Jerik, Proximate of the Interworld Council. In the three years Sael had been at the academy he had never seen a member of the Council except from a great distance, and then he had been filled with an awe he had never forgotten. Now the proximity of the world's two highest leaders was enough to root his feet to the floor.

They stopped about ten paces away and looked up simultaneously. *Flee*, Sael thought wildly, but he couldn't.

The proximate, Jerik, regarded him severely. In his midthirties, the proximate's brilliant Topaz hair contested for dominance with the piercing command of his fierce gray eyes. The power in his manner shook Sael's composure.

"You are in a restricted zone," he said. "State your purpose and authorization."

Sael's mouth went dry. Authorization? He had none! He wasn't even part of the academy anymore. His thoughts jumbled into fear and confusion. "R-Restricted?" he finally blurted.

3

The proximate's nod was barely perceptible as his gray eyes gripped the student before him.

"I wasn't . . . no, I mean, I'm . . . I'm going, sirs, uh, Councillors . . ." He turned away quickly, flushed with embarrassment, totally flummoxed. How could he have passed the zone?

"Wait," First Councillor Hedrick quietly commanded, and when Sael turned back, the elderly councilman was watching him intently. "What are you doing here?"

For a second time that evening Sael's emotions welled up. It was not easy to face the tall man. Despite Hedrick's advanced age, his angular features had not lost their nobility, nor did his silver hair distract from the startling clarity and statement of power in his black eyes.

"I . . . nothing, First Councillor. I mean, I don't know what I'm doing here." It was the wrong thing to say. Sael knew that immediately and avoided Hedrick's piercing look as he tried to rephrase it. "What I meant, sir, I was walking in the outer wing and lost track of things." That too sounded awkward, and he felt the warmth creep into his face. The first councillor's presence was disconcerting. "I had my thoughts elsewhere, sir."

First Councillor Hedrick nodded slightly. "Who are you? What is your class position?"

"Sael Torr of Lym. I, well, I was in class seven of the academy."

"Was?" Hedrick prompted.

Sael stumbled on, partly because he felt they really wanted to know and partly because he wanted to tell somebody. "It wasn't because I didn't want to fly space. I want that very much," he said, as if that justified everything. "But I could not force myself to go on another day with M'Goba. We don't have the same feelings about space, I guess, and we had . . . differences. I left his class a third kusha* ago."

---

* kusha: a unit of time equivalent to 1 hour and 45 minutes.

"Which brings me back to my original question," said First Councillor Hedrick, frowning. "What are you doing here in the restricted zone?"

"I wanted one last visit to the center before I turned in my band. I didn't know I had passed the zone. I was too absorbed in my thoughts."

The proximate, Jerik, was about to rebuke him—Sael could feel the man's glower—but Hedrick seemed to catch Jerik's mental attention, silencing the proximate before he could speak. Then the first councillor turned back to the young man.

"What is your rating, Sael?"

"High."

"I assumed that," Hedrick snapped, his tone unnecessarily harsh. "How high?"

"430 over 90." Sael answered, finding it hard to face the councilman for any length of time.

"With a ranking qualification for the center, what were you doing in class seven?"

Sael's look was contemptuous. "They placed me there for disciplinary purposes." Despite attempts to withhold the reaction, scorn for the academy instructors began to give way to an inner upsurge of tears, which Sael just managed to suppress.

Hedrick's eyes narrowed suddenly. He telepathed something to Jerik and motioned to Sael. "Come with us."

Dismayed but curious about where they were taking him, Sael followed the two councilmen, upbraiding himself for his stupidity at blundering into a restricted zone as well as for his emotional response, which he was sure they had sensed.

They led him along three more corridors and finally into an office. Austerely furnished, it held only a few chairs, shelves of books, a desk, and a small desk console. Emblazoned high on the wall behind the desk was the dark-blue space center symbol, elaborately intertwined with the intricate silver-and-green symbol of the Interworld Council, on which was engraved the Council Plan: WORLDS IN UNISON THROUGH JUSTICE AND WISDOM.

Sael slipped into the chair indicated by the proximate as the councilman sank into another. First Councillor Hedrick went behind the desk to the console.

"Student number?" he asked.

"47-2995."

Hedrick fed in the number, noted the readout, and settled back in his blue chair, studying the nineteen-year-old student. "Do you know exactly what your discipline problem is?"

Sael looked down unhappily. "I've been told a lot of things. M'Goba says I'm too outspoken. When I was in DeGoy's class, he said I was rash in my thinking. But I know it's my unstable nature. I get bored with the classes; then the drone gets on my nerves. I can't control my thoughts and explode emotionally when the instructors try to control me. They told me it could be handled in class eight-four, but it wasn't. I got worse. Then I was placed in class seven to see if I would respond affirmatively. I just dropped out of that class."

Jerik mulled that over. "I don't see why they didn't place you directly in the space center under a guided internship. Unstable or not, anyone ranking over 425 over 90 and in the top four percent has no business in those classes. Your emotional instability could have been handled well enough."

"They didn't think so," muttered Sael, hating whatever it was that made his emotions snap uncontrollably to the surface at insignificant things. Over the years he had learned to force the feelings down over minor incidents. But he had never had the discipline necessary to keep them continuously subdued, nor had anyone taken the trouble to teach him. One teacher had tried during his childhood. No one would attempt such base tactics to control him again. Sael was sure of that!

6

Hedrick telepathed a quick remark to Proximate Jerik: *"You know why he's not in the center. With his instability? I'll wager he's never had discipline training."*

"So? His emotions can't be that hard to contain. If he'd been placed in a guided internship . . ."

"Guided or not, Jerik, you cannot deny Sael's emotional instability is violent. I know you sensed that. But I will say one thing in his behalf: Considering his unstable nature, he must have some unusually strong percept open to him." Since Hedrick had met Sael in the corridor, he had found himself partial to the student and knew it was due to the young man's instability. Normal people were merely telepathic. However, unstables had additional abilities that threw their emotions into precarious balance and sometimes into strong, uncontrollable reactions. He resolved to find out what Sael's abilities were.

"Sael, this is a hypothetical situation. What are the quad flight angles in space between parallel sectors two and four?"

"Sir?" Sael didn't want to question the man but was a little unsure of what the first councillor was aiming at.

"If you are 430 over 90, prove it."

"The situation can be looked at in two ways: in hyperspace, which, in those sectors, would involve jumping the time warp, or in regular free space, where you have none of the random patterns you have to overcome in the frequencies of hyperspace."

At mention of the time warp Jerik and Hedrick looked at each other sharply and began rapid mental communications from which Sael was deftly excluded. Hedrick worked with the console again, telepathed something to the proximate, and turned back to the young man. "How do you know of the hyperspatial time warp?" The question was posed with deceptive mildness.

"I read a lot." The words were out before Sael had a chance to think. And once he had spoken, guilt rode him hard.

"You're over 430," Jerik said evenly, the fierce eyes no less severe than they had been in the corridor, "but that does not give you the option to lie."

Sael, though, did not hear the last remark, too caught up in the councilman's first words: "You're over 430." He stared at the proximate and then at Hedrick. "That's impossible," he stammered. "I was tested last week. Those were my results!"

"Did you see the scores?" the first councillor countered.

Something about his tone made Sael realize he had been almost shouting in the quiet room. He lowered both his eyes and his voice. "No. M'Goba told me."

"The results are on your graph. Your rating, according to your charts, is 483 over 90." He flicked the screen around so Sael could read it for himself and added dryly, "Which isn't bad, considering 500 over 90 is top rating."

Sael's mouth hung wide as he looked at the screen, and he barely heard as the first councillor went on.

"Even at that high a rating it would be impossible for you to know of the time warp. The only existing reports on it are sealed in my office in the Council chambers. And the only other people who know of the reports, to my knowledge, are the other thirty-four members of the Interworld Council and their aides, the first admiral of this space center, and the crew members of the *Silver Nebula*." He leaned over the table, his black eyes intent on the youth. "How did you come to know those reports?" The words fired demanded an immediate and truthful answer in return.

Sael sighed. "It's my power, sir. I can't control it, and half the time I don't want to. I was tested and found so unstable emotionally the instructors wouldn't allow me into the normal telepathy classes. I'm classified as a high instability risk." He fought against rising emotion again.

"Maybe I am," he continued, "but that's what gives me my power. At least that's what I figure. I suppose it could be anything, but I've heard unstables, especially high-risk ones, have definite tendencies toward excepttional abilities."

"Do you know the extent of your power, specifically, how it helped you come across those reports?" asked Hedrick.

Sael looked down at the plush blue floor, wishing Hedrick would stop questioning and do whatever he intended to do. "I don't know how far it extends. I can read past the mental blocks of most people without trying to, though not of exceptionally trained people like you, but I can get instant thoughts past just about any block. I also get brief flashes of places and objects. Once in a while I'll get complete fixes on them, enabling me to study whatever it is at my discretion.

"A couple of months ago I got a fix on those reports in your office. They were lying on your desk, scattered about somewhat, and no one was in the room at the time. How I ever got that fix I don't know. It just . . . well, it simply came. I wasn't even trying to get one, but since I had a complete fix on the reports, I knew what they contained. I guess I realized they were confidential. I never told anyone about them."

"Is there anything else you can do with your power?" Hedrick seemed genuinely interested.

Sael was silent for a moment, searching his percept. As usual, when he wanted it the most, it was unresponsive, although he felt something give way slightly. "I'm not sure," he said at length, still pondering what that something had been. "I've never been able to test its full extent, although I have—" He stopped abruptly and shut his eyes, trying to ward something off. His body went rigid.

The two councilmen reached out mentally in silent observation. The instant Sael felt their touch he quivered and shrank back, automatically shoving up a mental wall of such force it temporarily blocked them from entering his mind. No! They must not see it! He didn't want to see it himself, but there was no stopping the scene from unfolding. The image was there, stark and vivid as if he were part of it. Indeed, he seemed to be. But it couldn't be true!

Out of a tranquil sky a thunderous bolt roared down, struck, and leveled nearly one-third of the Interworld Council building. Other flashes began striking around him; he watched in horror as different edifices and areas of the city were hit and burned. A bolt streaked to the spot where he stood. He tried to jerk away. Emotion like the stab of a flame-ridden blade tore through him. Unable to accept it, he screamed.

Chapter 2

WHEN SAEL CRIED OUT, both councillors shoved against his mental wall in an effort to find out what was happening. They broke past it to receive only the final brunt of the emotional force he experienced.

"Sael!" Receiving no response, Jerik instinctively rose and went to the young man. The proximate had his hands firmly on Sael's upper arms and, now that the block was down, called to him mentally.

"Relax your thoughts, Sael. That's it, keep them steady. Just relax them and settle down."

Feeling the soothing communication from the councilman, Sael began to come out of it. The transition from the vivid mental picture back to reality was so smooth he hardly noticed what was happening. He sat quite still for some time, forcing himself to calm down.

"Sael, what was it?"

For the first time Sael realized Jerik had spoken telepathically. Instinctively the young man jammed up a new mental blockade, forcing the councilman out. He opened his eyes and focused them on the proximate. His body was unnaturally and uncomfortably warm as his thoughts jerked sharply back to the flashing bolts. He fought against the raging emotions inside, as bitter as the agony in the mental scene. He looked away.

"It's all right," Jerik said softly, releasing his hold on the youth's arms. "Just tell us what you saw."

"It is not all right!" he said, choking back tears and not wanting to face either councillor. How could he, after such an outburst? These men had every emotion under perfect control.

"What did you see?" The authority in Hedrick's voice brought Sael's head up and, painfully, an answer out of him.

"It . . . was horrible. I was in a field just below the Council building when suddenly there was a noise like the grating of two electrical field plates, and an energy flare from some ship demolished the building. Then there were others aimed at different areas of the city, leveling them, leaving the ground charred. . . ." He stopped.

"And?" Hedrick pressed.

"I don't know. That's all I got. It was too intense! I kept getting everyone's feelings. I felt them die!"

"When did this take place?"

"In the future."

"How far in the future?"

"I don't know. I couldn't tell!"

"Have you met with the future like this before?"

The questions tore at Sael's already ragged emotions, but he answered, knowing the first councillor would not pressure him needlessly. "Three times. The first thing I foresaw was the time you suddenly announced that Councillor Jerik was to be your proximate. The next time was the Battle of Morassu out in space. I saw Commander Taron get killed on that mission half a month before it actually happened. The third time was yesterday morning. I saw the same thing I saw today: the destruction of the city. Only I didn't get as much."

Hedrick regarded the young man. At length he said,

"I want you to let me enter your mind, and when I do, I want you to recall what you saw. Let me observe it with you. I want to see what I can find out about it."

"I don't know if I can do that. I've never recalled one with the original clarity before."

"I'll guide you."

"I . . . don't know." It was true, he had never been able to recall his premonitions with the clarity observed the first time, but he was more nervous about being in close mental contact with the first councillor.

"Look, all I want to do is find out what I can about your specific power and instability to determine whether or not this premonition will come true. Don't be afraid that I'm going to read you," he added with a hint of a smile.

"But the others were valid!"

"True." Hedrick nodded curtly, understanding Sael's concern. "But premonitions may be false, and without specific training you can't tell the difference. Will you let me enter your mind?"

Unwillingly Sael relented. Apprehension mounted as he felt the first councillor's powerful mind reach out to touch his. He shied away. It was hard enough to be face to face with the man, but the mere thought of contact aroused instinctive resistance. Sael tried to block the intrusion but found it difficult to counter Hedrick's power.

"Easy. I won't hurt you."

Reluctantly Sael lowered his blocks. Smoothly and almost imperceptibly Hedrick and Sael were in full mental contact.

"Show me what you saw."

If it had been his choice, he never would have looked at the thing again. The images were too vivid. It took some effort to bring forth the scene from the future, but it was clearer than any premonition he had ever recalled before, almost identical to the original. He forgot Hedrick was with him, watching it unfold. In fact, he nearly forgot that this wasn't actually happening, that it was merely a possible scene from a possible future as once again he caught the slicing emotion of the people of the city. It became a horrifying crescendo, threatening to overpower him again.

"*Enough!*" Hedrick's sharp thought wiped the scene from Sael's mind and snapped him back to reality.

Sael looked up at the first councillor, questions burning inside, none voiced for fear of the answers.

Hedrick sat back, smoothly breaking the mental connection, thinking not only of what he had seen in the premonition but also of what he had perceived during the brief contact with the young man. Unstable or not, Sael's intelligence was as keen as the graph stated; but his emotions were wild and his abilities were undisciplined. Hedrick doubted Sael knew half of what he was potentially capable of—whether his powers were disciplined or unmanageable.

"It is real," he said at length. "I have no doubt about that. What you have seen through your power is not a false vision."

"When?" Jerik asked quietly.

The first councillor looked at his proximate for a long time. "I can't tell for sure."

"Then it could happen tomorrow!" Sael burst out, forgetting whom he was with.

Hedrick shook his head. "No. It won't happen immediately. Your percept was very clear about when it was not. However, it began to get hazy as to a month away and very vague in two months' time. We therefore have up to two, maybe three, months to discover exactly what will strike us. By then we should be able to overcome it." He rose, indicating the discussion was closed. A slight smile softened the sharply defined mouth. "Thank you for allowing me into your mind. You've helped us more than you realize."

Jerik also rose and motioned to Sael.

Sael nodded respectfully. Was this it? he wondered. Would they let him go now, or were they taking him to some holding center for his earlier blunder of entering the restricted zone? As the three walked out of the room and into the deserted hallway, Sael, torn between curiosity and respect, asked the question that was foremost in his mind.

"First Councillor Hedrick?"

"Yes?"

"What did you find out about my power?"

"I wasn't in there to discover your capabilities, just what I could see while you recalled your premonition."

"But did you see any of it, sir?" Sael persisted, now having brought it out in the open. "I can't see it myself to even begin to understand it."

Hedrick stopped and looked at the young man before him. Jerik waited patiently beside him, also looking at Sael, as the first councillor spoke out. "Those who are unstable by birth are rare on our world and always have been known to command some special power. It can range anywhere from unusually perceptive telepathy to advanced telekinesis and beyond, and on rare occasions unstables have more than one channel open to them. Right now I see you have four major channels open to you."

Four! Sael stared at the first councillor.

"What you need," he continued, "is someone to help you discipline them. Here, let me have a sheet of paper."

Still astounded, Sael fumbled with his notebook, pulled out a sheet, and handed it to the first councillor. Hedrick took out a silver pen, wrote something in dark-green ink, and gave the paper back to him.

"You've never had formal discipline training, have you?"

"No, sir."

"Those"—he pointed at the paper in Sael's hand—"are the transport coordinates to the home of a very good friend of mine. He's an excellent teacher and also very strict, which is what you need if you ever want to gain any control over your power and instability. You'll find him free tonight, so go on over and have a talk with him. Try around kusha 4.4. He should be home by then. I'll tell him you're coming, and why, so he'll be expecting you. Don't let him down."

Surprised at this turn of events, Sael looked in awe at the first councillor. Councilmen, he knew from talk, had ways about them mysterious to others. They were highly regarded, even feared by the general populace for their tremendous power and mastery of it. Yet to be treated like this when he was expecting punishment for entering the restricted zone . . . "As recondite as a councillor" was a phrase he had heard often, and now he counld see its meaning, even if he could not understand theirs.

"Thank you, sir! I'll be there. But whom will I be addressing?"

"You will find out when you arrive. He doesn't like his name given out with his private coordinates. A person such as he deserves all the privacy he can get."

"He will accept me?" Sael knew the situation was not to be taken lightly, but his other teachers had been too willing to get rid of him.

"Would I have given you his coordinates if I weren't sure? Just do what I said. You'll be in good hands."

Sael nodded. "I'll follow your instructions, First Councillor Hedrick. My farewells, sirs," he addressed them both, then, pocketing the paper, hastened down the glistening corridor.

The two councilmen watched him leave. Then they resumed their walk, taking a different corridor.

"Interesting youth," Hedrick said after a while.

"It's too bad he dropped the academy. With his rating, he would have proved valuable to the center, not to mention the Council," said Jerik.

"He's an undisciplined unstable. You know why he was dropped." Hedrick's lack of concern annoyed Jerik.

"They shouldn't have pushed him from class to class, though."

"What else could they do?"

Jerik knew he was right. Most people of Sael's age were learning to fully master their natural telepathic abilities. But the young man had hair-trigger emotions and powers he could not comprehend, much less control. Undisciplined, he could not be allowed anywhere near the space center by the academy. He would have more frustrations than he could handle. Then one day his emotions would slip and he'd turn on someone without warning, tearing him to mental shreds. It had happened before. So they'd had to keep juggling him from class to class until he decided to leave on his own.

"It's still a nasty thing to do to someone like him," Jerik argued, beginning to like Sael.

"It's the only way to handle him easily under those conditions. He knows he's different, and he's trying to fit in where he knows he won't. That kid's got a tremendous amount of potential, and he's also extremely unstable. He needs someone who can control his outbursts, someone who can withstand anything he might throw out, and especially someone who will understand him."

Jerik nodded in agreement. "Whom did you recommend?"

Hedrick walked on for a few more paces, remaining silent. Then he turned to his proximate and simply said, "Why, you, of course."

Chapter 3

JERIK STOPPED AND STARED at the elderly councillor, refusing to believe what he had heard.

Hedrick eyed him steadily, waiting for the expected retort from his proximate. Receiving nothing but a slack-jawed stare of disbelief, he resumed walking.

The initial shock wearing off, Jerik hurried to catch up. "You really meant that, didn't you? You gave a totally unknown, unstable kid my number, and you expect me to teach him control?" His look plainly showed he thought Hedrick's age had finally affected his sanity.

"That's right," the elder returned.

"Look, I've got my responsibilities with the Council, not to mention those I've got with the space center . . . on top of which lies the threat that some intragalactic force is going to wipe out Lym, possibly all of Galapix! You can't just throw some unstable kid at me and say, 'Here, take him!'"

"Jerik, listen—"

"Listen to me, Hedrick. I know what he's got. I also

18

know the special kind of care and training he needs, and I can't give it to him. I don't have the time."

"Then you'll find the time, won't you."

"No, I won't. That's downright—"

"Just hold your silence a moment, will you? You don't know half of what Sael's got. He has more channels open to him than anyone I've ever come in contact with, with the possible exception of you. He needs training desperately. He has tremendous potential, and if he doesn't get the chance to learn how to use it, he'll drive himself insane. Then he'd really be dangerous."

"Turn him over to a regular teacher of the power, not to me!"

"It wouldn't do him any good. He'd react just as if he were in another class at the academy."

"There are teachers that can handle him!" Jerik insisted.

Hedrick shook his head. "I want you."

"Why? If he means that much to you, you take him in."

"I can't. He has access to the future, and I don't have that channel open to me at all or, believe me, I would."

Jerik looked at the first councillor for a long moment. Access to the future. It was beginning to make sense.

Hedrick went on. "If he gets flashes of things that are under top security, doesn't that make him important to you?"

Jerik nodded. It was virtually unheard of for anyone to have the ability to penetrate Council security solely with the power of mind perception, especially anyone not thoroughly versed in the operation of the Interworld Council. Incredible as it was to find a student of the academy with such an extraordinary ability, there had been a few such instances. Such students were highly regarded by the Council if they showed positive promise and if their emotions were not destroyed by their raw power.

Hedrick continued. "And what about his premonition? He had the same one you did about the invaders. Look, I'm not asking you to be his permanent tutor. Just get him to control his future channel. We know something is going to hit us. I need you to develop that power and work with him until we know *exactly* what and *exactly* when, so we can prevent it."

"But my future channel isn't that keen. What about Adia? She's got a sharp sense of the future."

"Her future opens up differently from yours or his. She never did get that premonition except as a dark spot of worry, and she couldn't get a proper fix on it. Maybe your channel isn't that keen, but you control it flawlessly. You have to get him to open his up, so we know what we're going to be up against."

"What if we're powerless against it?"

"What if we're not?" Hedrick's voice edged on impatience, his left hand gesturing upward. "We won't know until you find out. I'm giving you all the time you need to work with him. Days, weeks, whatever it takes. Consider it top priority. Understand?"

Still annoyed, Jerik nodded in wordless compliance.

"I want you working with him constantly. You might have him live with you for the first few days or so . . . until you get the premonition from him. Besides, it will do you good, after living alone all this time, to have some company other than those maintenance probes you have floating around."

"The probes are a good deal less trouble to look after than he's going to be."

"Nonsense."

"What about the Council?"

"I need you working with him right now more than I need you directly in a meeting. Besides, you are doing this for the Council." He paused for a moment, his black eyes searching out Jerik's. "You do understand the full implications behind this, don't you?"

Jerik knew the first councillor better, perhaps, than

anyone else did. Reaching out with his thoughts, he touched Hedrick's and found them troubled and unusually unstable. He had not known the elder to be in such disquiet for months. True, this was no abstract matter: The fate of his world rested on the premonition and undisciplined power of a young unstable and on Jerik's ability to cultivate that power and pull the premonition from him.

Jerik brushed lightly against the turbulence with cool, steady thoughts until all traces of worry vanished. "Yes," he said, answering the query, and then added, "If Sael is going to be looking for me tonight, I'd better get on, hadn't I?"

"I think that might be wise."

"I'll keep you informed on the progress," said Jerik, and he teleported to his home.

It was just kusha 4.4 when Sael finished dinner and changed clothes. As he slipped into crisp brown slacks and a tunic, he tried to imagine whom he would meet and could not think of anyone in particular. He probed his channels and wasn't surprised when they didn't respond; he hadn't expected they would. He went to his transport console, which was built off the small entrance hall, stepped on the pad, punched in the coordinates, and again was not surprised to find them locked against his transition after what the first councillor had said about his friend's leading a private home life. Customarily one signaled the person at the other end mentally before one transported or, if he had the ability, teleported, but Sael didn't know where to direct his thoughts or to whom.

Sael fed in the coordinates again. This time the connecting light shone, indicating the line was open. Setting the control, he braced himself. Steel-like darkness enfolded him as though he were shooting down the inside of a tube. Within seconds he was in an expansive foyer with white crystalline walls that arched to a lofty ceiling. Underfoot were hexagonal gold tiles with an abstract swirl of white in the glaze. Beyond, he could just see into a vast room with a rust-colored floor and beige crystalline walls that curved gracefully around out of sight. An elaborate wire sculpture spanned most of that wall. Constructed of gold and flax-metal treated with beige, black, and russet, the art captured Sael's attention.

It was easy to feel lost in the vastness of the mansion, and he wondered who could possibly own it. When Jerik stepped into the entrance hall from an opening hallway, Sael's jaw dropped even wider in amazement. He clamped his mouth shut and nodded a nervous greeting.

The tall councilman was wearing informal clothes and smiled affably at him. "You weren't expecting to see me, were you?"

"No . . . no," Sael stammered, "I had no idea I was coming here, Councillor."

"Just call me Jerik. I'm out of uniform. Besides, I don't usually request strict formalities in my own home. Are you ready to get started?"

"What? Now? With you?" The words tumbled out before Sael could contain them.

Jerik laughed openly, his unaffected manner putting Sael a little more at ease. "Of course now, and of course with me! But we're not going to do it standing out here. Come on." He led the way from the foyer across a sweeping room and up a short curving ramp.

Sael decided Jerik was easier to talk with than Hedrick had been. The first councillor was aloof. Powerful. Rigidly disciplined, true, but one didn't feel at ease with him. The proximate, on the other hand, despite his power, was more comfortable to be with.

They entered a small lounge with deep-set chairs and soft wall lighting. Elegant works in woods or metals adorned the room, which was decorated in soft beiges and unobtrusive greens with a plush floor, inset bookshelves, and a low ceiling.

Jerik sat down and watched as Sael looked around, wagering to himself that the young man had never seen

22

so elegant a private home. "Make yourself comfortable." He extended a hand to a cush chair. "Fix it however you like."

Sael sat down. The chair was firm. He adjusted the internal airflow knob on the armrest until the cushions were comfortably soft and sank back in the deep chair, smiling at the councilman. "This is great! But why did First Councillor Hedrick want me to come here?"

Jerik leaned back and looked at the young man. "He feels you have a certain channel open to you that cannot be ignored at this time."

"My future line?" Sael asked.

"That's right. I have a line to the future, too, and I received the same premonition three days ago, but it did not have the clarity yours had. See, we know something's going to hit us in the next couple of months, and if we're to combat it, we've got to know the exact details. You seem to have the clearest premonition so far. If I can work with you, help you develop control of that line, it would help the Council tremendously."

Anticipation shone in Sael's eyes. To be given such an offer by a member of the Interworld Council—to help the Council!

"So the sooner we start," Jerik continued, noticing Sael's reaction, "the sooner we discover what we'll be up against. Now I warn you these sessions may get rough. It is not going to be easy for you at times, but as long as you're willing to go on, it shouldn't be too bad. What I am going to do first is simply ride your channels just to see how far they extend, so I know what I'm working with."

Anxiety welled up. How rough was rough? Sael wondered. What did Jerik mean when he said it wasn't going to be easy? There was one thing he knew for certain: He did not want the councilman's powerful mind invading his.

Jerik caught the mounting fear. "Relax, Sael," he said quietly. Knowing the delicate balance of Sael's emotions, but not their limits, he waited until he sensed that Sael had lowered his rigid mental barriers and then slowly began to make contact.

Tentatively Sael allowed him in. Instead of a myriad of things concocted out of fear, he felt a refreshing coolness that allayed his anxiety. The councillor's first light contact grew stronger and more defined. Sael felt the control and precision with which Jerik probed. Before he realized it, he was watching the process in fascination and allowing the proximate to search deeper and deeper through the extent of his unstable emotions and power.

Only slightly aware that he was being observed, Jerik moved along the channels. Hedrick had been right: A vast array of channels lay open to Sael, and that, unfortunately, meant he was extremely unstable. Riding out the channels, he saw how the young man's life had been ruled by his eruptive emotions; his keen-edged intelligence overshadowed by his instability. Learning strict emotional discipline would be difficult, but Sael would have to learn it before he could gain mastery over his channels.

Easing out, Jerik thought long about it. True, Sael was exceptionally quick to learn, but with those volatile emotions . . . Above all, Jerik had to get the entire premonition from him. There were several ways to go about it, he thought, looking abstractedly at Sael. Some were crude and fast; others, easier on the person, took longer. Jerik knew he had little time to get the full premonition. On the other hand Sael had never had training. Use of a blunt method the first time might drive him so deep into hatred it would take months, maybe years for anyone to win his confidence again. Then again, it had its advantages. . . .

Jerik decided the first step was to test Sael's actual control. How well could the youth accept a disciplinarian's intrusion in his thoughts? More importantly, *could* Sael accept the basic action of a disciplinarian's suppressing his emotions?

Jerik doubted it. Still, he'd have to take that action to know for sure. He would have to get Sael to respond emotionally, then abruptly lock himself in the youth's reaction. It would be rough, seemingly unfair to Sael, but it was the only way Jerik could determine exactly how far Sael's control extended. Eventually the young man would learn to suppress the emotional response completely, handling the intrusion instead with mental blocks or his power, depending on the situation.

Unaware of what was going through the councilman's mind, Sael eagerly asked, "What did you find out?"

Jerik carefully chose his next words. "Before we can do any more with your power, you'll have to learn discipline, basically, how to control your unstable nature. You've let it control you for the past nineteen years."

Embarrassment and hurt surfaced involuntarily with the slight chastisement. "I couldn't help it!"

Without warning, Jerik's powerful thoughts whipped out, caught Sael's emotions, and moved deep within the reaction.

"Hey! What are you doing?" Hatred rose like fire in dry brush. Instantly Sael tried to barricade himself from the councilman. Jerik easily resisted his efforts. Sael lost his last measure of control and lashed out at the intrusion, more furious than he had ever been, determined to eject the proximate from his mind.

Calling on his power, Sael felt something open up and tried to channel his wrath through it. But something was wrong. It would not go through.

Jerik merely held his position steadily, irritating the young man all the more.

"Get out of my mind! Get out, get OUT!"

Now openly in tears, Sael tried desperately to pull away from Jerik's thoughts, strained, and in his attempt backed into the open channel—his future line. He became entangled in the premonition he'd received at the space center. The flash of light streaked toward him . . . he had to get away . . . NO! Jerik was blocking his only exit . . . ride it through . . . no . . . everything was a distorted, churning mass sliding into a vortex of agonizing emotion . . . the people dying . . . it was a vicious nightmare! He screamed.

The channel split open suddenly. Sael bolted for the exit. Once out, he caught flashes of various things, among them the fact that Jerik's thoughts were still invading his mind. Anger flared again. This time he would get him out despite all odds.

About to strike with the full force of his rage, he felt a sudden coolness wash over him, a soothing relief that simmered him down. Immediately he was ashamed of the way he had acted.

"I'm sorry, sir. . . . Please, I couldn't help it." He risked a look into the deep gray eyes and was startled to see them almost twinkle.

"You're a fighter, aren't you?"

"I couldn't help myself!"

"That's exactly what I meant. You've let your emotions run wild all your life and found you could always hide from them or threaten your assailant with them in the hope of frightening off who or whatever it was. I wasn't going to let you do that. That's why I made sure you knew I held onto your first reaction. You had to do something about that, didn't you?" He smiled gently, no suggestion of correction in his manner now.

"I tried to get you out, and you wouldn't leave. And then I tried to run, but there wasn't anyplace to go, so I backed into the open channel. I fell into the future again. . . . That was a nasty thing to do, Councillor."

"It was the only thing I could do, Sael."

"You could have warned me about it!"

"You think that when you're suddenly confronted with a situation in the future it's going to take the time to explain itself to you? No. You have to look at it and figure it out for what it is and handle it right then."

Wearied by the mental battle, Sael was too tired to argue. And, reluctant as he was to admit it, Jerik was right.

26

Sensing all this, the proximate nodded. "I think you've had enough for the first night. We'll start again in the morning. I'll show you where you can sleep, and then you can go home and get whatever you need."

"You mean I'm staying here? With you? Tonight?" Sael stared at him, flabbergasted.

Jerik chuckled good-naturedly. "Longer than tonight, I think. We can work out a good schedule with you here. Besides, I want to keep an eye on you for a while."

"Yes, Councillor!"

Jerik rose, rested his hands on his hips, and looked cockily at Sael. "Didn't I tell you to call me Jerik?"

"Uh yes, Co— Jerik."

Jerik flashed a wide grin. "Come on. I'll show you where you'll sleep."

Chapter 4

THE SKY WAS TURNING from midnight-blue to shades of silver-pink beyond the mountains when Jerik awoke the next morning. Dimly he wondered what had roused him at this early hour and was disgruntled when he found he couldn't get back to sleep. There was *nothing* more frustrating than waking up early and not being able to get back to sleep, he thought. He buried himself in the pillowy softness and found he was more wide awake than ever. Annoyed, he tossed back the covers and rose. He went to the eastern wall and switched on the window. A section of the wall slipped quietly out of sight, leaving a clear barrier between him and the outdoors. He flicked the switch again, and the barrier, too, passed back into the wall.

The night air had a chill snap to it. Shivering, he reached for a cloak and wrapped it about his body. He leaned his red-bronze arms against the sill and gazed out at the black outline of the mountains against the sky. The stars in their fiery brilliance were just beginning to fade, and all was perfectly still. Not a whisper of wind, not a tree or animal stirred.

He felt content to stand there, feeling the chill air against the warmth of his face, feeling the dawn. *This is what it must be like to be a star amidst the vastness of space*, he thought, *to be the first rays of sun yawning and stretching over the mountains and into the valley below.* Ever so gently he reached out with his thoughts to experience the sensations of dawn breaking.

He could feel it coming: slow, austere, yet scintillating with hidden sparks of the laughter of children romping on a golden hillside. The abrupt contrast and interplay between the two gave him the feeling of total freedom. As the sun rose, he rose with it, stretching out his sense of time so it would last practically forever. . . .

Suddenly, as if time itself had exploded, the valley was bathed in early morning light. Smiling, Jerik savored the flavor of the morning just one moment longer before he turned from the window. It had been a perfect sunrise.

As he dressed, his thoughts turned to the matters of the day and Sael. If he could get the full premonition from the youth, he could take it to the Council and get back to his work. Sael could then go under a regular tutor; there were teachers that could handle him.

Nevertheless, as he was pulling his tunic on, he paused for a moment, recalling how difficult it had been for him to learn the basics of controlling his own unstable nature. True, he'd had poor instruction and little help at first, but even under good circumstances it had taken a while. And Sael wasn't just any unstable. Aside from his broad range of powers, the young man had a brilliant mind, probably the only thing keeping him from unleashing those powers in sudden fits of rage when his volatile emotions flared to life. Jerik remembered the pains and torments he'd had as a youth, shuddered, and drove the thoughts back deep where they belonged.

He finished dressing and headed down the silver-yellow hall ramp, feeling its comfortable sponginess beneath his feet. As he passed the entrance to the main living room, a movement caught his eye. Curious, he poked his head in the doorway and found Sael in there, looking in wonder at the golden archwood carving that stood near the eastern wall. Jerik came up behind him.

"Welcome to the morning. What are you doing up this early?"

The closeness of Jerik's baritone voice when Sael had been expecting nothing made him start. He whirled and came face to face with the proximate.

"Uh, nothing. Why are you up?"

"I couldn't sleep."

"Neither could I."

"At all?"

"Well, I woke about a third kusha ago and couldn't get back to sleep, so I got dressed and came down here." He didn't mention that he had also taken a self-guided tour through the lower levels of the mansion, which Jerik suspected, anyway.

"Sleep well otherwise?" He smiled at Sael.

Sael nodded and returned the smile. "What's our schedule for today?"

"I thought we'd look into the future some more." Jerik felt Sael wince mentally and smiled reassuringly. "Among other things. But not before breakfast. Come on." He led the way into the kitchen.

"You know," said Jerik offhandedly while they were eating, "if you can find out when in the future this happens, we can easily take matters from there and handle things. That's all you need to do . . . find out when."

Sael was finishing the last of his frucchan, dipping the small lavender leaves in a thick warm syrup and letting the mellow flavor linger in his mouth as long as possible before swallowing them.

"But what about you? You said you had the same premonition. Don't you know?"

30

Jerik shook his head. "No. My sense of the future isn't that keen. Oh, I get premonitions once in a while and can usually pinpoint them, but only if I catch them the instant they flash in my mind. This one came on me so abruptly I didn't have a chance. The way you pull in that future line of yours, though, you should be able to get the date and time with no problem."

Sael looked at the councilman, wishing he could be like him: in flawless control of his power, emotionally stable, and sure of himself. But he knew he couldn't. He'd never be able to control himself. He would simply have to leave. The proximate's valuable time and efforts could not be wasted on him.

"*Ah, don't worry about that.*" Jeriks thoughts came through. "*It takes practice every day and, more importantly, exposing yourself to the wide variety of situations you have to handle.*"

Sael slapped his wall up. "Hey!"

Jerik shrugged and rose. "You had your mind wide open, and I was in proximity."

Sael's emotion's flared. "You were prying into my thoughts!"

"Nothing of the kind. You left them wide open, indicating I was welcome."

"You should have known those were private thoughts, and you should have left!" He rose, his green eyes vicious and his thoughts flashing to wild conclusions, as they always did when his emotions took over. Did this man have no discretion?

Jerik confronted him solidly. "People aren't always going to be that polite. Now sit down, and let's get a few things straightened out."

"So you can stick your meddling thoughts into my mind and . . . and . . . read me? Oh, no!"

"Sit down!"

Sael wanted to run but couldn't make himself move. "You're . . . you're using your power on me! Forcing me to stay here! I don't *want* you prowling around my thoughts. I don't want to have anything to do with you! I just want to get out of here!"

"Sit down."

For a moment Sael just glared at the councilman. Then, without thinking, he bolted toward the open door.

Not about to let Sael get away that easily, Jerik teleported to the doorway, blocking his escape.

Sael halted in his tracks and stared at Jerik, who just stood there, eyeing the young man evenly.

What with the impact of witnessing for the first time someone teleport at close range, and unexpectedly at that, it took Sael a moment to recall that the proximate was a teleporter and another moment for blistering anger to override his astonishment. How could he have forgotten?

"You deliberately read my thoughts that I was going to run and ported to block me!" He rushed at Jerik in blind rage.

Jerik grabbed him by the arms and found Sael more difficult to hold onto than he had expected. He had a feeling Sael was using more than physical strength, whether or not he was doing it consciously. "I didn't have to read you. I could see you were leaving!" He gave Sael's arm a sharp twist.

Muscles taut, Sael struggled vainly against Jerik's grip. He kicked at the councillor.

For a moment Jerik felt an ancient rage spark inside. He forced it down. That was just what he didn't need at this time. "Settle down or I really will read you, and you won't like the procedure either!"

"Just let go of me!" Another solid kick flew and connected.

In a flash Jerik was in the young man's mind again to divert his attention from kicking to trying to attack mentally. The mental assaults Jerik could withstand. The blows he wasn't sure about.

Sael fell for the trap. Forgetting physical activity in

an effort to get the councilman out of his mind, he concentrated on throwing all his energy at Jerik and searched his channels for one he could use. He brushed against something. Hoping for an outlet, Sael blindly channeled himself into it. Horrified, he realized he'd hit on his future line again. As the gripping scene unfolded, he was unaware that Jerik had slipped into the channel with him in silent observation of what was happening.

The sleek black ship plunged into space from out of nowhere, shuddered slightly as it emerged, then stabilized and moved toward Galapix. It unleashed a barrage of fire that accumulated increasing energy as it sliced through the planet's force shield and atmospheric layers.

He saw the Interworld Council building and watched as a bolt struck the magnificent edifice. There were blinding flashes all about; the emotion of the people whipped through his awareness and blackness began to overcome him. But wait! Hadn't Jerik said that if he could find out when this was to happen, the Council could prevent it?

Sael pressed at the enfolding darkness. Not that he cared about Jerik, of course, but there was the rest of the Interworld Council to consider, not to mention his own future and the future of the people.

With agonizing pain the web of darkness eased away, and the full force of the future struck him again. When, he asked himself, when?

The attack continued until the city was devastated. Once the task was complete, the ship moved off, picked up speed, and seemed to waver before it vanished. Sael looked at the ruins of the city. His thoughts flashed back to the ship, wondering where it had come from and where it had gone. Then, with lightning fury, the full implications of the premonition became intensely clear. It hadn't been just any ship from some other planet. It was—

"*No!*" he screamed. "Nooooooo!" The truth was so unbearable he blacked out.

Jerik himself perceived the force of the premonition as

Sael became unconscious. The thought was staggering, and only the sudden heavy weight of Sael's limp body in his arms drew him back to reality. He turned his thoughts toward the young man and realized that his unconsciousness was deep. Sael would be out for a good four kushas. Without further thought Jerik adjusted himself to the weight, dutifully took the youth to his room, and laid him on the bed. Jerik's thoughts were already bent toward the Council and what he must report. Sighing, he teleported to the assembly room of the Interworld Council, where a session was already in progress.

Faintly Sael heard someone calling his name and, not wanting to be coaxed from the comforting blackness, he was annoyed.

"*Sael!*"

There. Now he recognized the voice and felt angry: It was Jerik again. He tried to slip back into his darkness. After all, it had been the councilman who had caused all this in the first place! He'd forced him to hit the wrong channel and stumble into the future again. Well, he wouldn't come to while Jerik was still around.

"*Sael, please!*"

The coaxing was very gentle, and Sael was too tired to resist it, so he came back to full consciousness, making certain his mental blocks were firmly up. He didn't want the councillor probing around his thoughts again!

He groped with his hands, realized he was lying on a bed, and opened his eyes to a darkened room and Jerik standing over him.

"What am I doing here?"

"When you lost consciousness, you really lost it. I brought you back to your room, and you've been lying here for nearly five kushas." He looked quietly at Sael in the dim light.

"No thanks to you," Sael grumbled, sitting up.

"What do you mean?"

"You're the one who started all this. You're the one

who made me go into the future and get caught in that channel!" His temper churned furiously.

Jerik's thoughts washed coolly against Sael's wrath.

"Quit that!"

Jerik sighed and relaxed his thoughts, easing them away from Sael's. Next time he might just let the kid wallow in his mental muck. "When you hit the future, I followed you."

"You did what?"

"I followed you."

"See? You were prowling around my mind again!"

"Settle down," Jerik said wearily. "For one thing, I was not prowling around in your mind. I don't make it a habit to go snooping in other people's private thoughts. What I did do was link myself up to your future channel when you were receiving the full premonition. I had to get all the information I could on it. Don't you see? If we don't find out *exactly* what's going to happen, we are going to be in for an attack on Galapix, and we won't be able to do anything about it! Not a thing!"

Chapter 5

JERIK SANK INTO a chair, his head down. Sael looked at him in the low light of the room. The elaborate silver-weave uniform Jerik wore appeared inconsistent with the suppressed emotion and worry Sael sensed emanating from the proximate. Councillors didn't worry about things. They handled matters, but they never worried about them.

"What did you find out?"

Jerik looked up slowly, blanketing his feelings. "What about you? What did you find out?"

"I . . . well, I . . ." Sael was quiet for a while, remembering. Feeling. Shuddering. "That ship," he said.

"What about it?" There was no trace of hidden emotion in the councillor's manner now.

"It wasn't just any ship."

Jerik reached up and adjusted the wall lights back to their normal level and sat back in the chair. "Go on."

"The time warp. It rode the time warp from the future."

Jerik nodded.

"It wasn't from just any future either, was it?" The youth's eyes were wide with fear.

Jerik watched him, alert for any sign of emotional outburst.

"That ship came from our own future, didn't it? Maybe a hundred or so years from now, but it rode the warp back through time to destroy Lym now . . . to destroy the Council, because by doing that, its people change circumstances, altering the course of *our* future to fit *theirs*, setting conditions up for their own black time then!"

Jerik nodded again. "In that future a very few key people control the government. They control access to the future and the past by means of the time warp and mean to exert their control over as many other worlds as they can. Galapix as we know it now doesn't exist in that future. After the destruction of Lym, order will be lost and people will have lost much of their telepathy or will have rechanneled it on different lines. Those who have unstable natures, like us, are killed, or they reach the most advantageous positions of power and brutally wipe out the weaker ones. You are quite right. It is a very black sort of world."

Sael gave Jerik a suspicious glare. "How do you know all that?"

The councilman smiled. "Once you know how to read your channels properly, you can find out quite a lot."

Read whose channels, Sael muttered to himself. "Did you see when, though?" was what he voiced aloud.

"What about you?"

"Well, you know more about it," he retorted. "You saw—"

"Hold it. It's your power, remember? I only went along for the ride."

Why did Jerik have to put it that way? Sael sat back on the bed and closed his eyes. "I don't know. I remember it was sometime in the very near future. Like a couple of months. Six days before the month of Gor, I think. Yeah, that's what it seems like." He opened his eyes again.

Jerik was smiling faintly. "Very good, Sael."

"You mean I was right?"

Jerik nodded. "But knowing that isn't enough. We need to know exactly at what point they leave their future to come back into this time."

Sael looked confused. "But why?" he started to ask. Then understanding lit his angular features. "You're going to ride the time warp!" Excitement overrode his turbulent thoughts. "You're going to try to stop them from coming back into the past!"

"Now you see why it's so important to know precisely when they leave their future."

"But when is that?"

"See for yourself. It's your premonition."

"Jerik!" Sael protested, not wanting to confront it again.

"Look." The councillor's face grew stern, his high cheekbones becoming more defined. "It's *your* channel. *You* have to find out what happens in it."

"Well, you just read my—"

"That's enough. Get back in there, and find out when they leave their time." Mentally he gave Sael a gentle prod.

"All right!" Sael snapped. "I'll do it. Just don't push me into it."

He closed his eyes and probed his channel. It was dark and unresponsive now. He knew it would be.

"*Press harder. Go at it as though you were really looking for something.*"

"*Hey, I told you to stay out of my mind!*"

Jerik ignored the remark. "*Listen, keep a firm pressure on it, and it will open up for you. You can manipulate it if you keep the pressure constant. Guide yourself right into it ... there. ...*"

Without realizing it, Sael was in the channel again.

The premonition swiftly ensnared him. He cried out involuntarily.

"Keep pressing!" The councilman's steady thoughts seemed to come from a great distance. *"Don't let yourself be scared off by it, or you'll never get anywhere,"* he encouraged.

"But . . . but how . . ." Encasing him completely, the channel distorted and closed itself off. Sael fought back the growing panic of being locked in.

Something very firm held onto him now, stabilizing and helping him shove the channel back in shape. Soon he had control back.

"Now get to the beginning of it," said Jerik, *"and direct your whole attention to finding out everything you can from that ship. In reading your channel, you're simply gathering information from it as you would from any book. If you have the power open to you, you'll find yourself pulled toward what you seek. Don't shun it! You will know the answers to the questions you pose."*

Oblivious to everything, Sael concentrated on the sleek black ship. When was it from? When? He tried to receive even the tiniest impulse or thought and managed to latch onto something very vague. Try as he would, though, he could not get it to clear. It was too far away, too difficult to read.

Dejected, he backed out of the channel, feeling the councilman still watching him. Sael didn't want to face Jerik after his failure.

"Sael?"

"What?" he mumbled, looking at the mottled gold-brown floor.

"Sael, look at me," Jerik said quietly. He waited until the young man glanced up. "What did you get?"

Sael looked away from the piercing gray eyes. He admired the steadfast patience of the man and was ashamed of his inability to see what must have been very plain. "I don't know," he mumbled. "It was so vague I couldn't read it properly."

"When do you think it was?" Jerik asked gently, the cadence of his voice bringing Sael's head and eyes up to meet his again.

"I don't know. Maybe 157 years from now."

"How many months?"

"I don't know."

"What did it seem like?"

"Maybe two. Three. Three, I think."

"Days?"

Frustration raked through Sael. "Jerik, you're asking too much. I can't see beyond that!"

The councilman nodded, releasing his visual hold of the youth. "Don't worry about it. You got the year and month pinpointed."

Sael looked at him in growing wonder. "You're not just saying that, are you?" he said slowly.

Jerik shook his head. "Precisely 157.3372 years into the future. I found that out when you hit your channel earlier this morning. While you were unconscious, I took the opportunity to inform the Council of exactly what we are up against. We know what we're dealing with now, and we know that in order to make a start toward handling this, we will have to jump the time warp into the future so that our future, not theirs, will be preserved. We must prevent their coming back into the past to destroy Lym."

"Can't we stop them here when that ship emerges into our own time?"

"Think, Sael. The optimum time is before they leave their era. If we wait for them to come to our time, they will destroy not only us but the Interworld Council as well, not to mention Lym. Although the premonition does not indicate how one ship could devastate our fleet, it is not false. That *will* happen—*if* we wait. Our only chance is to meet them before they enter the time warp. Stop them at the source before they can enter other times as well as ours. But . . ." He sat back thoughtfully.

"But what?" Sael persisted.

"What then? We have to play it by ear. We don't know how we're going to stop them or what we're going to do because there's no telling what will happen when we do arrive in the future . . . if we can ride the warp at all. How are we going to prevent such a thing from happening again? There is very little we do know, aside from what sketchy information was in the premonition." Jerik was thinking out loud now, hardly aware that Sael was still listening to him.

"I don't suppose riding the time warp beyond your mark and learning about the future after it has already happened would be of any help, would it?" Sael broke in. "I mean, all you'd have to do then is look back at past records to see everything you wanted to know. . . ." He hoped this was a good idea.

Jerik shook his head. "Risk getting caught in an even more dangerous future than what we already must expose ourselves to? Sael, they're not going to improve with the years when they change our future to match their liking." His voice was soft, his eyes intent on the young man.

"Our future will become so barbaric we wouldn't recognize it even if we did get that far into the future, and we shall not. We can find out what we need to know when we get into their time"—he grew thoughtful once more—"if we make it. There are a great many unknowns to overcome. . . ." Jerik slipped into silent pondering, leaving Sael to watch him.

That had been foolish, Sael thought, and wondered why he had brought it up in the first place. After all, the proximate obviously knew the wrongs and rights of the situation and didn't need any discharged academy student to tell him how to run the warp. Withdrawing into his thoughts and unknowingly increasing his susceptibility to receiving flashes, Sael was aware of nothing but troubled thoughts until a flash suddenly sparked in his channel, snapping him alert. Vicious! Unthinkable! But utterly accurate.

"Jerik!"

The urgency in Sael's tone pulled the councilman from his thoughts.

"Someone's going to kill y—"

The words were lost in a sudden burst of violent physical energy. Sael's head swam. As nothingness enveloped him, he lost all sense of balance and was falling . . . falling. . . .

A scream tore at his throat, yet there was no sound. He could see nothing, feel nothing except the awful sensation of spinning in an eternal fall.

Then, abruptly, he found himself standing whole and alive in an open meadow. He looked around wildly and was sorry. The world spun around, and he fell to the ground.

Jerik reached down with a steadying grip on the young man's arms, his eyes meeting Sael's with calm intent.

"W-What h-happened?"

"We ported out." Jerik watched Sael quietly for a time. "You okay?"

"Yeah, I think so. Is that what it's like to teleport?" Sael wasn't at all sure he wanted to experience that a second time, even if it was the only way to get back.

Jerik shook his head. "It's a lot smoother than that. I haven't teleported anyone else for nearly a year, and the last time I had time to prepare myself for the extra load."

Sael looked around. "Where are we?"

Jerik looked at the area, a grassy clearing encompassed on three sides by forests of everdark timber. The mountains surrounding the meadow rose precipitously above, while on the open edge of the clearing the woods banked down a steep gully, leaving an unhindered view of the mountain range beyond and the valleys below. Somewhere water fell in a cacophony of distant thunder. The air was still, the sun bright in the early morning sky, whereas it had been midday moments before.

Jerik shrugged. "I don't know. Probably somewhere in the Tieke Wildwoods."

"You been here before?"

"No. I just ported to the first place that came to mind." He sat back in the deep meadow grass and gazed up at the intense turquoise sky.

"But the Tieke Wildwoods are hundreds of leagues from here! I-I mean, from where we were."

Jerik watched three silver-orange birds cross the sky and disappear into the forest beyond. "I know." He couldn't help smiling.

The smile was too broad to go unanswered, though there was awe in Sael's voice when he asked, "How far can you teleport?"

"As far as I want to, I suppose. As long as I can get a clear mental picture of an area, even if I've never been there, I can port to it." He lowered his gaze from the sky and towering mountains and fixed it on Sael. "But we have other things to discuss right now. Like who was going to kill me and how."

"Didn't you get my message?"

"I got your warning, all right." He was about to add something, thought better of it, and changed his mind. "But by then I was porting here."

"I had a flash that someone intended to kill you with a sudden transfer telepathy, someone who is living now but has strong connections with the future—not *our* future, but the altered one. Whoever it is was trying to stop you from completing your plans. I got the impression that this person is one of those who plan to start the disruption of the Council system in three months—after the attack."

"In other words, taking over in the midst of all the confusion and then, while nobody's looking, jumping in and raising havoc with the government, which is to be expected," Jerik murmured. "I don't doubt that by now others have received that premonition. The Council can keep some things under tight security, but as far as premonitions go . . . that's something we cannot keep from others." As he thought about the flash Sael had received, he absently ran his fingers through the grass. The soft, resilient slender blades felt good in his hands.

As a matter of good practice, Jerik kept up extensive mental screens to prevent others from attacking him in a sudden, overwhelming transfer telepathy, and it was, in fact, part of the reason why he had not originally received the flash.

In picking up the young man's urgency, he had swiftly forced a duplicate flash and had seen more in it than Sael had. Sael had not perceived that the attack was aimed at him as well as the proximate. Normal blocks were one matter, but not having security block discipline, Sael was vulnerable to that assault.

Teleporting to an instantly thought-up location was, in Jerik's estimation, the surest way to confuse the enemy. Let the person attack empty space, he mused. He scanned his channels for some clue to the origin of the assassination attempt. The proximate frowned and took a thorough look through the duplicate flash. There was no indication of who the assailant was, just a killing thrust of energy. Jerik saw with surprise that it had been violent and abrupt enough to have ripped through his own blocks. Attack telepathy worked best on one person. It took someone skilled in all aspects of telepathy to attack two people simultaneously, and at best that was a difficult maneuver. The assailant must have had good knowledge of the proximate to know how to direct the attack, but Jerik couldn't tell who it was. The flash hadn't been any help in that respect. Yet there was a vague, almost disturbingly familiar feeling to it. The proximate wondered if he was being observed by the assassin again, but he could not find that out by flash or any other sense. The attempt on his life must have unnerved him more than he knew, and he intensified his blocks to prevent another possible attack. He'd tell Hedrick about it.

The fragrance of the forest and the subtle odor of the wild yrthi growing in profuse colors made him want to forget everything and lose himself to the mountains. A cool breeze broke the morning stillness, waving the grass into ripples and wafting the intoxicating yrthi their way.

He forced his thoughts back to the matter. "I've got enough mind shields to guard against such attacks," he said, deciding not to tell Sael the rest, "but thanks for warning me anyway." He smiled.

Sael looked vaguely startled at the acknowledgment, having expected, rather, a reproof. He smiled.

"Jerik, you said as long as you can get a clear picture of a place, you can port there."

"Mmmmmm." He nodded.

"Well, how do you get a clear picture if you've never been there? Like this place?"

"It just comes. It's getting a fix on something, is all it is. You just get it, right?"

The inflection in Jerik's voice pointedly reminded Sael of his flash of the time warp reports.

"Or if you have a little discipline, you just put one there. If you can get clear fixes on places without ever having been there, you may also have the power to teleport, as," Jerik added, "you do."

Sael was suddenly eager with anticipation. "You mean it?"

"Yes. But I think we should be getting back."

"Now?" Sael was dismayed. He didn't want to leave the meadow so soon.

Jerik grinned, realizing the yrthi had affected more than his own senses. "We have a lot of work to do with you back home. You don't want to be unstable all your life, do you?" Until that moment the councilman had thought that once he'd had the premonition, he would turn Sael over to a regular teacher of the power and get the youth

45

out of his way. However, not only had he grown fonder of Sael than he thought, but he recognized the young man's vast potential, which just any teacher wouldn't be able to handle.

"Couldn't we continue out here?"

"It's too distracting. For me as well as for you." He looked up into the turquoise sky again, thinking of the stars beyond in the forever night and of the black ship from their own future coming back to destroy Lym. They had to stop that ship in its own time, he thought, and to do that, they had to ride the time warp, something never before attempted. Although the warp had always been a bother to navigate around, it had been only three months since the discovery that it was actually a bulge of the time continuum into hyperspace itself. The reports had been kept strictly confidential. Yet Sael had seen them with his power—by design, or was it merely accident? Jerik wondered. Certainly the young man understood the phenomenon as well as any who had seen the reports. And that intrigued Jerik professionally.

"Sael," he said slowly, bringing his gaze down, "how familiar are you with the operation of the big ships?"

"I've never interned on them, but I've been in enough classes to know something." He grinned.

"I expect you have been." He looked intently at Sael. "Listen, we've got a flight scheduled later this week to begin our experiments with riding the time warp, perhaps to make the warp run itself. I want to arrange it so you can be on that ship."

Sael caught his breath, scarcely daring to believe the proximate.

"Understand, the reason why I am doing this is to give you some experience on how they operate. That and . . . well, with your range of power you might turn out to be very useful to me if we did make it into the future."

"Useful to you? How? You mean like my warning you about the attack?"

Jerik couldn't help smiling at Sael's eagerness. "Perhaps. I don't know yet. But if I'm ever going to consider taking you with me, we've got to get to work. You are still unfamiliar with your abilities, and you are still unstable."

Sael suddenly grew serious. Jerik felt the abrupt shift in his manner and watched him carefully. Even something as simple as calling him an unstable could set off a reaction inside the young man, but this time it was not what he expected.

"Jerik, do unstables ever become truly stable without having to worry about their emotions ruling their lives?"

The answer was brief and conveyed gently. "No, we must guard our emotions and bury the vicious ones. We can never be like the others."

Jerik was relieved when Sael's only reaction was a nod. "But we can come awfully close." He smiled. "Are you ready for teleporting?"

Sael looked at him uncertainly. "It's not going to be as rough as it was before?"

"No. And I want you to watch how I go about it so you can see how it's done. You've got a wide porting channel open to you. Since we've got the premonition out of the way, I think we should begin to expand on some of your other lines. Are you ready?"

Sael nodded and stood with the councilman.

Jerik had been right; it went much more smoothly this time. Although Sael's balance still twisted out from under him, that lasted only a moment before he found himself back in Jerik's home. They stood in the living room. To their surprise First Councillor Hedrick was there, waiting for them.

Chapter 6

"WE'VE MOVED UP THE flight," said Hedrick. "You're scheduled to break orbit at kusha 2 this afternoon."

Jerik sat down and stared at the first councillor. "But I thought—"

"After you picked up the total premonition, we decided this matter had to be handled immediately. You're to consider yourself back on Council duty, in command of the *Silver Nebula* this afternoon."

Jerik knew it was the only way. Like all the council members, he knew the black vessel had to be stopped. Since they knew nothing about riding the time warp, experiments might take longer than any dared anticipate. Still, there was Sael to consider. Something that went deeper than Jerik's vast mental channels wanted him aboard ship. He motioned toward the young man. "I want him with us when we make the warp run," he said decisively.

"What? As undisciplined as he is? Out of the question."

Listening in hope, Sael felt his emotions rise against the first councillor on this turn of events. He fought them down, knowing Hedrick would never allow him on board if he made a display.

Hedrick did catch the flare-up and pointed it out to his proximate, proving his point. "Look at him now, Jerik. If he can't control his emotions in a simple situation like this, how do you expect him to react when he's under pressure aboard ship? You can't just let him go up there with you. Even if his emotions were bridled, he's never interned on a ship."

"He's a 483 over 90. That's higher than most of the techs we've got working on it."

"They have two main advantages over him. They've got experience, and they're not unstable."

Jerik did not need to look at Sael to see the youth's determination to make it up to the ship for more than his own sake, and the proximate felt his own anger toward Hedrick begin to well up. "Pressure is one of the best cures for lack of discipline. Put him in a situation where he must use his powers or die, and he'll learn control."

"Just what do you want him to do? Man your free flight?"

"Of course not. But he could be valuable to me with his abilities!"

"And dangerous as well!"

"We have only fourteen on board that ship with any sort of power at all beyond the norm."

"They cover a wide range all together."

"Not single-handedly, though! I want him—"

"That's enough," Hedrick snapped, gesturing abruptly with his hand. "I have said it was out of the question, and I have said all I will say on the matter. You are relieved of your training duties with him, and you will be on that ship at kusha 2 without Sael. Have I made myself clear?

"Yes, sir."

Hedrick cast a sharp look at the proximate and then said, "I need you now at the space center. There are several matters I have to discuss with you before you leave."

Jerik nodded stiffly, then, catching a surface thought from Hedrick, said, "You know I hate the transport. I have to get Sael out of here first anyway. I'll port in."

Hedrick nodded in return. In a few moments the electronic transport from the center locked onto him, and he vanished from the room.

Jerik sighed. Sael just sat, not moving, not showing any outward sign of the torrent of emotions he felt, which Jerik could clearly sense. The proximate did note the incredible effort Sael was making to keep his emotions subdued.

Sael's self-discipline, showing maturity he had not expected of the young man, surprised Jerik. Emotional control for an unstable was difficult at best, even if one had had years of discipline training.

The room was silent. Then the councilman made a gesture of apology.

"Sael, I know how you feel. I said I would see if I could swing this for you, and I couldn't. There just wasn't enough time. Still, I have a feeling you are going to be vital to me on that ship, and I'm going to get you up there despite what Hedrick says. I don't know exactly when, but by the time he finds out there won't be a thing he can do."

"You really mean that?"

"Would I be risking my career on it? Yes, I mean it." *I may end up in court for this,* he thought, *but, Sael, we need you on this mission. I can't see how yet. But I feel it. I know it!*

"I have to go," he said aloud. "Block your thoughts from everyone as best you can, but leave a private line open. I'll most likely contact you in a hurry, and you will be porting again."

Sael nodded.

Jerik stood, took a moment to compose himself, and ported out of the room.

Sael sat back glumly, wondering about the future and what it would hold for him should the Council handle the mission. He supposed he could go back into internal tech, but he had never liked that. He couldn't go back to the academy. That was certain.

More than anything he had wanted to be part of the space center, to fly ships for the Council, and (if he proved himself worthy in his work) perhaps to be accepted as a special aide to a council member or, his boldest thought, to be chosen as a member of the Interworld Council itself. It was a dream he'd had all his life. Now the chance to fly for the Council had come so close, and it had been thwarted by the first councillor's flat refusal of Jerik's request.

Still, Jerik's insistence on getting Sael aboard the *Silver Nebula* bothered him because he knew the proximate could be permanently deposed from the Council for willfully acting against the first councillor's orders. Hadn't the proximate himself said he was placing his position in grave jeopardy? That was an enigma. Jerik was willing to risk his career on account of him! Not wanting to see that happen, Sael thought about refusing to go when Jerik called him. But if Jerik teleported him, he would not be able to refuse.

Running his fingers absently through his dust-blond hair, Sael sighed heavily and shook his head. When things started happening, he was always bypassed by the real activity and in the end stuck in the same rut. And, to get back to his original query, what about the future? Would it hold more of the same failed goals?

Curiosity began to override his depression. He approached his future channel in much the same way he had earlier in the day and pushed at it. Even with great pressure, the channel was unresponsive. Sighing again, he turned to his other channels, probing them as Jerik had done. Exactly what powers were open to him? he wondered—an old question. Leaving depression behind, he sought out the various channels with the new knowledge he had acquired from the proximate.

He came across a wide channel that he pressed at. It was the one he received fixes in, he realized. It remained dark and unyielding for all his efforts. Stubbornly he continued to press, forcing it open. Eventually a glimmer formed. It stretched out, became distorted, and gradually stabilized. A fix, and he had brought it about solely on his own! Although it was still vague, he'd done it.

Eager now, he explored it further. What was it? Rather, where was it? The image began to waver, and Sael struggled to keep it under control. There . . . he had it now: the back garden of Jerik's mansion. He could see it clearly, perfectly! Excitement growing, he wondered if channeling all he could muster at the image would make it possible to port there.

He tried. Concentrated very hard. Pressure built up explosively. Sael tried to remember how Jerik had ported, but the effort shook his concentration. He had to get out of that channel! As he tried to back out, he was horrified to find the channel had locked shut. The strain went beyond toleration. . . .

The world exploded in a burst of violent physical energy. His internal sense of balance went haywire, and he was falling . . . falling . . . twisting down . . . down . . . down. . . .

With a solid jolt Sael came to a halt and, dazed, slowly opened his eyes and looked around. Lofty trees and lavender hedges surrounded him in the stately court with its manicured moss-green lawn and crystal fountain gurgling soft water chimes.

He had teleported from the room to the lawn out here without anyone's help! Elated by the triumph, he shut his eyes, searching for the channel again, found it, and hunted for a fix. Again the channel was unresponsive; but Sael kept pressing at it, and presently a glimmer formed, wavered, and then stabilized. It was his own home across Lym. All effort went into concentrating. Not sure exactly how he had done it before, he would have to make himself part of the fix before he could port there, it seemed. He strained. The channel closed itself off. He was stuck in it again. Intense pressure built from within, and there was only one way out. That was to go all the way through.

Energy exploded in a burst, though not as violently as before, and his equilibrium slipped. For a moment he was overtaken by nausea as nothingness enveloped him, and then he stood in the small living room of his own house. Sael looked around and grinned, wondering what the proximate would think about his discovering how to teleport on his own.

A gnawing sensation in his stomach made him wonder at first if he was feeling an aftereffect of teleporting until he realized he had not eaten since early morning. A glance at the clock told him it was seventeen points* after kusha 1 in the afternoon. The lateness of the day surprised him. He went into the kitchen and fixed something to eat.

Everything was cleaned up by 4 points to kusha 2, when he thought about the proximate again. Having heard nothing from him, Sael pressed at his fix channel, trying to direct it toward the space center. A flash came, and with firm intent he steadied the picture, careful this time to stay out of the channel. He wanted only to look, not to be there.

Jerik was talking with First Councillor Hedrick; Hedrick's top aide, Kol Lenn; and Councillor Adia in the small private office in the space center, where Sael had been the evening before.

Adia, a strong-featured, insistent woman, whose hair

* point: a unit of time equivalent to 1.94 minutes. There are 54 points in a kusha.

was tawny gold and whose eyes were dark and fiery, was arguing against a technical decision of Jerik's. Both Hedrick and his aide were pressing her to end the dispute. Jerik, unwilling to move from his position, had half a communication line out to find Sael. The young man wasn't at the mansion. That bothered Jerik because it indicated that Sael now knew how to teleport, a dangerous move the first few times for one unguided. His attention veered from Adia's discussion with Hedrick and Kol Lenn, and he rapidly scanned his channels for a fix on the young man. Jerik was relieved when he picked up Sael's presence in the youth's own home across Lym, although he disliked the idea of Sael's experimenting with teleporting without guidance.

Adia, deferring at length to the proximate's decision, turned to him. "Well, I suppose you're ready, aren't you?"

"Mmm?" Jerik murmured absentmindedly. "Yes. I've been waiting for you to agree with what we originally had in mind without constantly changing it." However, his inner thoughts were projected to Sael on a specially blocked line. *"Listen, I'm going to port you very soon now, so don't move from your position or I won't be able to get hold of you. It's going to be close."*

Kol Lenn's eyes narrowed in sudden suspicion. "Jerik, don't you think you should have your attention *fully* on what we're doing?" Although he had sensed the blocked communication, he had not been able to read it or to detect the person at whom it was directed.

Hedrick, alerted by his words, could. He glared at his proximate. Jerik had already severed the line, but it was too late.

"I warned you about that!"

The proximate said nothing.

"About what?" Adia gave Jerik a sidelong look.

Hedrick continued, ignoring her. "This afternoon I gave you an explicit order, which I see now you had no intention of carrying out."

Jerik confronted him with unwavering intent. "I want him on this mission because he has a range of power that—"

"That he doesn't know how to control!" Hedrick flashed back. "You, above all people, know this is no assignment to entrust, even partially, to a raw unstable! I don't care what his rating is or what special power he has. You were given a direct order not to take him."

Adia stared at the proximate. "You were going to jeopardize this mission by taking Sael aboard ship? Have you lost all reason?"

"I have not," Jerik snapped, knowing perfectly well she had already made a wild inference about a situation she knew little about.

Kol Lenn, a short middle-aged man whose only ability ranged into deep-penetration telepathy, eyed Jerik carefully. "You are aware, Proximate Jerik, that willful disobedience of a direct command by the first councillor is a court offense, especially when it concerns a mission of this import."

Jerik bristled. "I am fully aware of Council law."

Hedrick spoke almost simultaneously with Jerik. "Kol Lenn, your recent promotion to my top aide does not give you the authority to address any member of the Interworld Council in that tone."

Kol Lenn bowed his head in deference to the two men.

Adia, however, hadn't had her final say. Jerik felt the slicing cold of the junior councillor's attitude through her professional veneer. Why she tried to cover it up was beyond him.

"He should not be allowed up at all," she told the first councillor, as if Jerik were a proved criminal. "If you release him now, he's going to find some way to get that unstable aboard ship. No undisciplined unstable should be on that ship under any circumstances. I can command."

"Absolutely not," Hedrick said, the authority in his strong, clear voice closing the discussion instantly. "Jerik commands. You know as well as I do he has to be on that ship. There is no reason why I should remove him or, for that matter"—he shot Kol Lenn a sharp look—"place him in a court action. Jerik has been warned. That is all this situation warrants."

Hedrick turned back to Adia. "Your duty, as far as Jerik is concerned, is to carry out *his* orders, assist him in whatever course of action he deems best. *Observe*"—he stressed the word pointedly—"his actions and give me a full report on them upon your return."

He faced his proximate with no less firmness in his tone. "Don't place this operation in further jeopardy because of your emotions. You're losing control right now, and I warn you against doing something you will later regret."

Jerik said nothing. The first councillor's statement about his emotions was all too true.

"I suggest you both get up to the ship and get started. See to it you do not teleport Sael up with you."

Adia was triumphant. Jerik noticed it, but forced himself to let it ride. He would have enough time on the ship to pit his will against her arrogance.

Unknown to them, Sael was watching through his channel. Angered at the decision, he knew it was up to him now to get aboard that ship. Jerik had said he would need him.

Thrusting forcefully at his porting channel, Sael gained a fix and launched himself into the channel with fierce determination. The picture began to clear with agonizing slowness. The bridge of the *Silver Nebula* . . . yes, that was it.

Silver-blue walls. Twelve stations in the elongated, hexagonal room. Faint metallic odors masked by the input of fresh air. Five female and three male crew members manned eight of the stations. Sael felt the vibrancy of both ship and crew.

Jerik and Adia entered from the turbo lift and went to their stations. Sael could see the room clearly, knew

56

its temperature, was aware of its exact moment of existence, yet it was still far away. He didn't know whether he could teleport that far. But he did have a fix on it. Sael concentrated. Strained. His body shook violently with the effort, but that didn't matter. He had to reach that ship!

He was straining against something. Was it distance? Or possibly somebody's block? He realized with increasing desperation that he had to get through the channel. Something gave way. He pushed harder. It gave more. Suddenly the image distorted and blurred. Without knowing what might happen if he teleported on a blurred fix, Sael thrust himself completely into it with a final burst of power. Darkness shrouded him. With overwhelming violence, the world shattered about him. He spun soundlessly in blackness, weightless and disoriented for what seemed like infinity. Then his body shuddered, convulsed violently, and hit something solid. Sael knew a brief moment of shock, then nothing.

Chapter 7

"SAEL? SAEL!"

Something touched Sael from a very great distance. Reaching toward it through the oppressing blackness took too much effort. He sank deeper into the silent dark, away from pain and reality.

"Come on, Sael."

The thought was sharper, more intent. It kept nudging him. It wouldn't be ignored. It would have to be pushed away . . . far away . . . so he could rest in the safe, close blackness.

"No! Listen to me! Hold on!"

Hold on to what? Sael thought, annoyed. The persistent intrusion was irritating. He started to fight against it. Shove, that's it, just shove it away so he could go back to sleep . . . fight . . . get it out . . . *no* . . . NO! Agony shot through the blackness. Positive the intruder had caused it, Sael screamed suddenly, trying to fight it with his mind. "NO! *Get out! You're hurting me!"*

"Come on, Sael, just a little further."

The thought was very gentle. Sael was suddenly confused. Where was he? What had happened? His head felt as though it had been blown apart from the inside out, leaving only bloody fragments. An attempt to move made him sick; it was as if he were out of balance with the normal universe. He cried out again.

Strong hands grasped his sides firmly, keeping his body still. *"You're just disoriented, that's all. Relax."*

There was the vaguest sensation of lying down and two people standing nearby. With great hesitation, Sael opened his eyes to a blurred universe, where up was way off sideways and down was all askew. Afraid of what had happened, he shut his eyes against the distortion. Pain blazed in his head so suddenly he screamed again. What was wrong with his vision? Oh, how his head hurt. And what had happened to the world?

The hands on his sides gradually released their grip, and he felt a coolness wash over his tormented mind. Another mind entered lightly, felt for the pain, found it, and drew it from him. The headache was gone, but the world was still awry.

Some time passed before Sael dared to open his eyes again, and when he did, the two forms standing near him were still dim and blurred. "W-Where-Where am— What's happening?" he stammered.

"You're on the Silver Nebula *in sick bay,"* came a quiet thought.

It was the same one that had coaxed him from the darkness, and suddenly it was recognizable. "Jerik!" Sael peered through the fog at the dim figure and simultaneously felt as though he were falling. Instinctively he grabbed the edges of the platform he lay on.

"Relax, you won't fall." Jerik's thoughts smoothed against Sael's, steadying them. The surgeon standing alongside the proximate also reentered Sael's mind with added stability.

The elements in the room gradually became defined, and as the nausea subsided, the two slipped unobtrusively out of his mind. Jerik telepathed a request to the surgeon, who nodded and left him alone with the youth.

The councilman stood quietly beside the platform for some time before saying anything. "You didn't tell me you knew how to teleport without help."

"I-I didn't . . . I mean, I couldn't . . ."

"I'd like to know how you knew I couldn't teleport you up here and how you managed to port this far the first time," Jerik said mildly.

Sael found it difficult to confront him. "I didn't know . . . well, I mean, after you left the house, I started probing my channels and found one wide open, so I pressed at it and got a fix on your backyard. I threw all my strength into concentrating and remembered how you had done it, and I teleported there. It wasn't easy."

"Then?"

"The next fix I got was my home in southern Lym. I concentrated again and ported there. That was easier than the first time. I grabbed something to eat and then became concerned when you didn't contact me, so I got a fix on you, First Councillor Hedrick, his aide, and Councillor Adia just before you sent me your message. When you cut off the communication, I suspected the worst. I knew you wanted me with you, so I tried to get a fix on the bridge. Then the fix wavered. I just threw myself into the channel in order to make it."

Jerik's eyes narrowed. "Never teleport on a wavering or blurred fix. That's one of the surest ways to blow yourself apart. Literally."

Sael glanced about the tiny room where he was being kept and decided it was better not to think about what he had almost done in his ignorance. "How long have I been out?"

"Almost three days."

"What!" He sat up in astonishment and was immediately sorry. Waves of nausea returned as the bed spun beneath him.

Jerik helped him back down. "Yes, you were out nearly

three days. Even Raien couldn't get through to you, and he's one of the most competent surgeons on Galapix—or off it. I finally managed it because I've been in your mind and know where you hide when you black out."

Sael looked away, still feeling ill.

"When you were porting," Jerik went on to explain, "you exerted so much force on your unclear fix you almost overshot your landing. You went so far beyond your natural controls that when you tried to compensate, you almost literally twisted your body inside out. You were fortunate to have made it at all. We slipped into free flight just after you hit the bridge."

He did not tell Sael that by the time Councillor Adia had informed Hedrick and Kol Lenn of the young man's appearance on the bridge the ship was already in hyperspace with the flight pattern locked in. There was nothing anybody could do. The warp experiments were more vital than the unstable, Hedrick had informed them, and contrary to Adia's and the aide's advice, the first councillor insisted that the proximate remain in command. That considerably eased Jerik's thoughts on the matter.

Jerik looked down at the young man and repeated, "You should not have attempted teleportation without knowing what you were doing. You could have permanently distorted your sense of balance, been blinded for life, not to mention torn your body apart."

"I'm here," Sael said defiantly.

Jerik smiled. "I'm not going to argue that."

"When's my equilibrium going to straighten out? It is going to, isn't it? It isn't permanently—"

"No. But it will take a good deal to straighten out. Raien will take care of that."

"What about you?" Sael wasn't sure he wanted someone else probing around in his mind.

"That's out of my line. I could no more straighten your line of balance than I could straighten a flax-metal bar with my hands. Besides, he's good. Straightened me out a few times."

"You've been disoriented, too?" Sael could not picture this man doing anything imperfectly.

"Certainly. Don't worry about it. He'll have you back in shape." Jerik turned to leave, and Sael, something still on his mind, called out to him. The proximate turned back, his gray eyes framing a question.

"Jerik . . ." Sael spoke hesitantly, as though afraid to tell the councilman what he wanted to say.

Wordlessly Jerik established a sense of safety, willing to accept whatever the young man would tell him.

"Kol Lenn and Councillor Adia wanted to place you under arrest for trying to bring me here. Since I came on my own, what's going to happen now?"

Sael's question caught Jerik off guard. Certainly the first councillor understood that the young man had ported on his own determination. Sael's porting had been as surprising to the proximate as it had been to the others. But that didn't mean Hedrick had to like it.

"I'll probably get a reprimand—nothing more. Hedrick won't run a court action for it, and Kol Lenn and Adia can't persuade him on current evidence. But you've no business in other people's matters simply because you have the power to establish fixes on them. You should have flatly disregarded that fix once you saw it was of a personal nature."

"But why did you insist on bringing me and risking—"

"That is not your business." Yet Jerik noticed a feeling of concern that he had not guessed Sael had.

"I am the cause of it," Sael said, as if that had given him the right to know more of the matter.

For some reason Jerik felt the same way, and he stood for a long time in deep silence. "Hedrick is wrong," he said at length. "He thinks we can do perfectly well without you aboard. But he's wrong. I feel it. Only fourteen of our two hundred and eighty-seven crew members have power beyond telepathy, even if only minutely, and out of those fourteen only three have any great variance in their power: Adia, Raien, and I. Suppose a situation were to arise where we needed someone with a vast array of powers? Or someone besides myself who could port? What then? The conditions are far from normal. We've never ridden the time warp before. We don't know what to expect from it. Now I know you don't know much about using your powers, but if a situation should arise in which I needed your extra power in some capacity, I could guide you. You might have to go through one of my channels, too."

Sael suddenly felt a mental ridge shoot up. Something still made him leery of the councilman, even though he told himself he trusted Jerik. Sael could not think why he felt that way and knew it was wrong, but the distrust would not be shaken.

Jerik sensed the ridge and understood it. "Will you open your mind to me?"

"Right now?" Alarm grew as Sael saw there was no way to get out of it.

"Yes. I want you to know something I cannot explain any other way. I have to show it to you."

"I don't know." Sael considered. This man had tricked him before. "Will you get out the moment I say?" He looked at Jerik uncertainly.

"You have my word as proximate of the Interworld Council. My word has been kept unbroken throughout my term."

Sael felt guilty for having made the councilman give his word, but he told himself he had to be certain. "Okay." He relented. "I'll open my mind."

Jerik nodded, and his gray eyes locked with the youth's pale-green ones. Spires of fear raced through Sael as the proximate's powerful thoughts reached out to him, and he wanted to break the contact; but before he could do anything, Jerik's mind had smoothly joined with his.

Sael felt as though he had been transported to another world in another time. He saw Jerik's own struggle with his instability as a boy and how it had raged uncontrolled for many years. And then how, growing up, he had been brought to a teacher of the power and forced to learn the basics of strict discipline, always fighting, resisting, and intensely hating those who had dared encroach upon his channels or thoughts. His instructor had given up on him. He'd been taken to another teacher and still another before one was found who thoroughly understood the power and internal struggles that made him so unstable, who could guide him with wisdom and mutual trust. It was this trust Jerik wished to convey to Sael. His deeply troubled youth was something he let very few see. In sharing this, he allowed Sael to enter his own mind and search out any hidden distrust.

Sael reached hesitantly toward the invitation. Curiosity drove him on. Once inside Jerik's mind, he found a refreshing calmness that felt sane and wholesome. It felt good. He began to understand why Jerik had let him explore his mind in such a way.

He brushed against a wisp of thought aimed at him, and he started, not expecting it. Looking at the councilman, Sael was perplexed to see Jerik eyeing him with a hint of amusement, and he looked for the thought again. It was gone, and the proximate's mind was no longer open.

"What was that?" he demanded.

Jerik only smiled at him. "Some things you have to be very quick about if you want to catch their full implications," he said. "I think you have seen enough for now anyway."

"But what was that?"

"In time you'll understand. Take my word."

Sael didn't know he had brushed up against a glimpse of himself as seen through Jerik's channel. But now that didn't matter. He had seen something far more important. He knew the councillor understood him. He understood the councillor. And what was more, for the first time in his life, he trusted someone.

Chapter 8

ONCE SAEL TRUSTED JERIK, he willingly allowed Raien to use his professional power to straighten out his sense of balance. After that was over, he began to spend more time observing the operation of ship and crew and less time worrying about his emotions. Jerik was used to having Sael on the bridge and became almost concerned when the young man wasn't there. He had reason: Though Sael's emotional control had improved, he still had outbursts at times and was easier to control when he was nearby.

When First Councillor Hedrick discovered the young man had managed to teleport aboard ship, he made the proximate solely responsible for any attack Sael might launch at the crew or anything he might do that, even indirectly, would contribute to the failure of the mission.

Jerik thought about that while reviewing with Adia the plans for the time warp flight scheduled the following day. It was unlike Hedrick to ignore his request.

". . . You're not listening, Jerik." Adia's voice sliced neatly through his thoughts, and he glanced up.

"Huh?"

"Will you get your attention back on what we're doing?"

For the past seven days her acid tone had been edging past his guard, trying to prod his emotions into the open. He didn't realize he was glaring at her until she spoke again.

"Jerik..."

"Quit it, will you? I know what we're doing tomorrow. We don't have to go over it a fourth time!" She was pushing him too far. She knew the plans, and he knew she'd requested this private discussion merely for the chance to rake him over.

She shrugged. "If you want to screw us up in the time warp, that's your business. Mine is making sure we get through it in one piece." She tapped a long finger on the notes they'd been going over. "Which we won't if you have your attention on that unstable all the time."

"We'll get through it in one piece all right if you watch your free-flight console reactions and handle accordingly. That was the sloppiest hyperspace jumping I've seen you do. You had better straighten out your mental and get it into sharper focus with the helmsman than that!"

"When you mentioned it to Hedrick, he didn't seem worried about my performance."

"Hedrick is not in command of this ship," Jerik said coldly.

"You shouldn't be. I don't know what came over you to ignore Hedrick's order!"

"Sael has, I will remind you, a tremendous range of power that I feel we are going to need."

"Well, I've sensed nothing of the kind."

"No. You wouldn't. Prejudices don't allow the senses to see in clear perspective, especially when it comes to foresight."

"That can be taken two ways, Jerik," she said meaningfully. "Hedrick wouldn't allow him on board, I've

66

sensed nothing. . . . You could be seeing only what you want to see. You see yourself in Sael, don't you? A wild, untrained youth with a range of powers and a chance for something you didn't get until it was almost too late.

"And don't try to tell me Galapix's future rests on him. He can't control his emotions to rationally use powers he doesn't even know how to handle! He's the snagging focal point in this whole operation, and if he botches everything up with a wild thrust of his power once we're in the future, it's your responsibility! You knew you had no right bringing him on board."

"I didn't *bring* him on board. He came on his own, and if I hadn't helped him through when he was porting, he would have blown himself apart physically. He was straining—"

"If you had blocked him, he wouldn't have made it."

"No, he wouldn't. He'd have been scattered all over his house. I couldn't let that happen!"

Dark eyes flashing and face set, Adia rose from her chair, shoving it back with a force that went beyond anger. "You could have altered his fix!" she exploded, unable to tolerate his glib answers any longer.

"He was fighting too hard! Changing his fix would have smashed him apart just as if I had blocked him. He'd never ported that far before." Jerik's gray eyes were fierce on her. "If you knew anything about porting, you would have done the same thing."

"I tried to stop him."

Jerik thrust himself out of his chair. "Well, it's a good thing he made it because if he hadn't and I found out your kinesis prevented him from making it through, I would have put you up before the court."

"For what? Don't threaten me with a court action. You're the one who's got it wrong about that . . . unstable!" She spat out "unstable" as though it were a filthy thing of which she had to cleanse herself.

Jerik walked slowly around the desk and stopped in front of her, fighting down an erupting torrent of emotion, not knowing how long he would be able to control it. "You are really going to do everything in your power to see that I ruin this mission, aren't you? You're testing my limits. You're going to pull at me until I give way, then stick me up before the Council and pretend you had nothing to do with it."

"You said that. I didn't."

"It's the truth, isn't it?"

She turned from him. Jerik grabbed her slender redbronze arms as though to release his emotions through the grip and forced her to face him again. "You won't admit it, will you?"

"Let go of me or I will make you let go."

"Yes," he said slowly, "you would, wouldn't you. You'd use your power illegally against another council member."

"I wouldn't talk of illegal actions if I were you. You don't have any say in this matter!"

As he released her, she pulled away and headed toward the door. The force of his grip hadn't hurt. She'd seen to that at least.

"Adia . . ."

She stopped but refused to look at him.

"All I'm asking is that you don't jeopardize this mission further by gouging at my emotions. If I give way, there's no telling what may happen." His voice was barely audible.

She whirled on him. "Then that's your own fault, Councillor! If you can't control your emotions, you have no business commanding this mission!" The contempt frozen on her face amplified the hatred blazing in her eyes, and the tension in the room held them both immobile. Then, cloaking her fury tightly about her, she left the room.

Tension snapped inside him as the door closed. Rage flooded all sane thought, and he was on the verge of porting after her when he realized what he'd been about to do. *No!* He couldn't let that through! *Control*, he told himself, biting it down in his mind, *even, steady control. S-t-e-a-d-y . . . down, force it back down . . . down. . .*

Weak and still shuddering, he sank into one of the cush chairs, burying the barbaric thought that had somehow surfaced from depths where such horrors were kept hidden, hoping to forget it, but it would not be easily or soon forgotten. He *had* wanted to kill her, to shove the horrors of thought into her mind, entwining her in them and obliterating her. He felt cold at the thought.

He was still trembling when Sael ported into the room. Sael looked at him anxiously. "Jerik! What's happened?"

The proximate looked up. "What are you doing here?" he snapped.

"I had a flash you were in trouble. Something was awfully wrong. I came to see what was happening."

"*Never* make other people's private business yours and violate their privacy every time you get a little flash! You'd better learn that right now! Get out of here!"

"But I saw you—"

"It's not your concern!"

"Jerik . . ."

The proximate rose, towering before the youth. "Leave."

Sael stepped back a pace in fear. Jerik's raw force burned through him with more violence than the young man had ever experienced. It held him rooted to the floor, and he knew he couldn't move if he wanted to. A tremendous blanket of pressure formed against his thoughts.

"I said, get out of here!"

"I-I-I can't. Honestly."

The councilman took a step toward him, his hands up, threatening. Then, realizing what he was doing, he stopped and lowered his eyes. "Just . . . just leave me, Sael. Please." His hands fell to his sides, and he turned back to his desk.

"Jerik, I'm sorry. I couldn't help it when I got the flash."

Jerik sighed heavily and looked back at the youth, his

hand reaching up to brush a lock of hair from his forehead. Why did the kid keep getting these flashes? Powers were strange, often unpredictable, especially flashes or premonitions, and he needed no warning from Hedrick that Sael must be kept under strict watch. But why this kind of personal stuff? "What did you get?" he asked at length.

"It was a sort of dual flash. There was so much hatred in it that it almost overpowered me. Not just from you, but from Councillor Adia, too."

"Were you actually searching for a flash at the time?"

"No. It just came. I couldn't stop it."

Jerik was quiet for a while, his thoughts heavy, as if burdened by a tremendous weight. "Sael, I'll handle it. Just don't go porting into other people's business anymore. Bypass those types of flashes. They're personal and none of your business. Ignore them. You think you've got that?"

Sael nodded respectfully and teleported out of the room. Jerik, too, left the room, on foot. Walking did have its advantages. It gave one time to think, and he needed those extra few points before facing Adia again. Coming at last to her cabin, he signaled at the door. He received a standard telepathic query in return.

"Adia, I have to talk with you."

There was a sudden ridge of hostility in her thoughts. *"On ship's status only."*

"It's vital."

"State the nature of this matter."

As if she couldn't guess, he thought grimly. She wasn't giving him any room tonight. *"Not if we are going to communicate about it in this manner. Let me in to see you."*

"Port in, then, if it's that urgent."

Jerik remained calm as he teleported to the other side of the door. She sat in an ice-blue cush chair, its color matching her attitude.

"What is so urgent you have to come in here? I know of no alert—"

"There is an alert in progress right now, Councillor, between the two commanders of this ship." The crispness in his voice silenced her. "I ask that you listen to me on the basis of your membership in the Interworld Council, not in the light of our argument."

Adia sighed and waved petulantly toward a chair. "I can see you're not going to leave me alone unless I do. So far I don't see what this has to do with the ship's status."

He sat on the edge of the chair and watched her intently. "Simply this: If we get into violent disagreements with each other, we are neglecting our duty to efficiently handle this crew."

"So?"

"Hear me out. You're guilty in this as well as I am. We cannot afford to let our emotions run wild and jeopardize the crew as well as the mission. I became so enraged I wanted to kill you. I've never let my emotions run like that. Not for years anyway."

She looked at him blandly. "I know. I got your thoughts."

"Don't you understand? I really *wanted* to kill you. It wasn't just a passing whim. I couldn't feel anything else!"

"Then why don't you do it now and get it over with?" she snapped.

"I can't. For the same reason you couldn't kill me."

She stared at him.

His voice dropped to a whisper. "I read your thoughts just as you read mine. I couldn't help it. They were too vivid. Adia, we have to face reality. Deep down we're still as emotionally unstable as we ever were."

"No!"

"You can't run from facts! You are unstable, and nothing can alter that!"

"That isn't true!"

"It's buried, but it's still there. Face facts, will you? If you didn't have your emotions so heavily sedated and suppressed behind your walls, you would do something really horrendous to me right now—wouldn't you?—as you wanted to do not five points ago."

With great effort, Adia drew a blanket of control over the emotions that had begun to surface at Jerik's outright statement. "It is not true."

"It is. You cannot deny that inwardly you are still unstable."

His eyes held hers. Both were silent for a long time. Everything in the room melted into oblivion as their thoughts merged. And thought-melded like this, she was no longer the acerb, self-assured person she had been a few points before. Her thoughts faltered.

"I don't deny that...."

"Then realize we both have to clamp down our feelings about each other if we are to get through this mission. I knew what I was doing when I tried to bring Sael on board. Hedrick didn't understand, and I didn't have time to explain. But Sael will help us. I don't know how, but I feel it. I am asking you to trust me and accept him."

"You're asking me to violate Hedrick's command! I won't do that!"

"Adia, the kid's already on board! Nothing can change that now. Accept whatever help he offers, and trust me when I say he will offer it."

Adia slowly broke the mental contact and turned away from him. Obviously, nothing could be done about Sael being on board. But as for trusting Jerik . . . Finally she capitulated, but with private reservations.

"I trust you," was all she said.

It was enough for Jerik. He rose and left the room.

Chapter 9

THE PRECEDING SEVEN DAYS had been filled with tests calculating the exact speed and vector angles of entrance into the time warp. Now, on the eighth day, they were ready to begin maneuvering into the warp. Jerik was in tight mental communication with his bridge crew and with Sael. That was not planned; but Sael kept slipping into his mind, and rather than expend energy blocking him, Jerik allowed the young man to remain as an observer.

Their first run at the warp was disappointing. The ship bounced over it, thoroughly shaking up ship and crew. Precise calculations were made anew, and the run was attempted again. And a third time. And a fourth.

The failure to enter the time warp was baffling. It was clear that penetration was possible because they had seen it in the premonition. But they were not penetrating.

Jerik sat in the white command chair, scowling. He slammed his hand down on a control, releasing a small field lock, rose, and strode over to Adia's station. He scrutinized her board.

"934 degrees," he muttered. "934. That's got to be the entry angle. It's got to!"

"That's what you said before," she murmured, "but it wasn't."

"Do we head up 939, Councillor?" asked his front-board navigator, ready to lock in the controls.

"939 degrees isn't going to make it. Anything beyond 934, and we flatly miss the warp. It's got to be that."

"917."

Jerik turned and found Sael looking at him intently. "Explain."

"I received a flash that 917 degrees is our entry angle."

Mentally forcing a flash duplicate of what Sael had perceived, the proximate examined it thoroughly. Adia, he knew, was doing the same.

She glanced up at him and, reluctantly accepting the validity of Sael's flash, said, "It's worth a try."

"917 degrees would bring us around to an awkward entry." Jerik glanced at the panel. "But I'm willing to chance it. The only thing I'm concerned about is straightening out and holding our course once we're inside the warp." Jerik paused, searching for a flash, then sighed to himself. "We know the potential of its pull, but we won't know its actual power until we get in there and find out. I don't intend to pull a reverse-course heading unless I have to." He altered the setting of several levers. "I'm putting it at 917 straight in. Then swing around to 039 degrees once we're inside, heading out again at 917. Helm, give me your direction readout."

"Course heading reads 4103."

"Free-flight engineer. Yours?"

"Free-flight pattern holding at 4.996.7."

He rechecked the board before he moved back to his chair. "Adia, don't overshoot the time line. It will be touchy."

She nodded. Sael went back to his seat, locking himself ˙nto it as Jerik sounded the warning shipwide.

They braced themselves as the great ship slued around,

not knowing whether to expect penetration or failure. And if penetration, what would the effects be on ship and personnel? They didn't have long to wonder. The ship hit the warp, and without warning, something violent and blue streaked through the bridge. It whipped around wildly, temporarily blinding those it approached. It touched Councillor Adia, who lost consciousness. Her body lurched against the controls on her console. The ship, out of control, plunged into the warp.

As the time warp expanded, they vaulted further and further into the future. Instinctively Jerik ported to Adia's console and shoved the controls down. The overload indicator glowed red. The ship did not respond. He thrust the levers back up and rammed a thought to the helmsman.

"Helm, give me the reverse line up on 254 degrees manual override!"

A split moment later came the response; *"1016."*

"Free flight?"

"9.014.8."

"Lock in and close on my signal." Jerik switched three levers, altering the board's combination and at the same time shoved a tense thought into their minds. "NOW!"

In unison, three pairs of hands locked the course into the ship. It shuddered with bone-jarring, oscillating violence. Jerik braced himself.

"Balsk," he telepathed to his helmsman, *"brake! Now!"*

The *Silver Nebula* strained against the braking maneuver. Pressure built up on the outside of the hull to the critical level.

"No response, Councillor!" The helmsman's thoughts were taut under the strain.

"Keep with it! If you let it slip, we ride this thing to the end of time."

The pressure began to change. Something was giving. Jerik hoped it wasn't the hull. Then, with a last sudden jar, they burst free of the warp.

After checking the ship's main life-support system,

Jerik went to help Adia. She was out cold, her nervous system badly damaged when the bolt streaked through the bridge. He wondered what it had been—a compressed energy field? Jerik looked about the room, checking on his bridge crew. Some were still fumbling at their stations, half-blinded. He telepathed the ship's surgeon to come to the bridge. Jerik's attention turned lastly to Sael, who stood straightening his green tunic.

Sael saw the councilman eyeing him. "I'm okay. The field lock snapped on me, though."

"I'm surprised most of them held," Jerik murmured, his attention already off the young man.

"When are we?"

Jerik shook his head and turned to the bridge crew. "I want a complete damage report and an immediate check on life support. We've got internal leakage somewhere. Pinpoint it, and seal those sections off."

He looked at the main viewing screen. The stars were familiar enough. They had been thrown a good distance from their original entry point outside the solar system. At least they knew where they were. But when were they? What did this time hold? he wondered, turning back to look at Adia. She was gone; Raien had already taken her to sick bay. Jerik moved back to her console. It seemed sound. The free-flight engineer working at the next station looked up at him.

"Status?" Jerik murmured, still working with the board.

"Our chronometers burned out—specifically, the link that establishes them with our movements in relation to outside time. My guess is that it was due to the initial jolt that passed through us rather than the time ride itself."

"Estimation on what that jolt was?"

The engineer shook his head. "Energy, as far as I've been able to determine. A specialized compressed-field energy. It gave my board a couple of unusual burnouts."

Jerik's look demanded a fuller explanation.

"The chronometer links don't give way under any kind of stress," the free-flight engineer continued. "That flight should not have affected them."

"We weren't under just 'any kind of stress.' It could have been the time flight."

"No, sir. The links blew when we hit that energy."

"Can we figure out when we are?"

"We're missing the data. We might be able to make an estimate with a lot of hypothesized calculations, but I doubt we can get an accurate account from that."

"How does it look for repair?" Jerik nodded at the control board.

"No problem, but I can't guarantee it won't burn out again. The rest of the board is okay except for a few circuit repairs, and I'll need someone to help me realign it in conjunction with the primary free-flight panel."

"Get with it then."

Jerik turned to Sael. "Can you handle Adia's panel?"

"I should. I've worked on models and seen it in operation."

Jerik nodded. "Idosh will need someone working with him to realign his board links. It hooks up through that console, and since there's nobody manning it right now, you might as well get in there and put yourself to some use."

"Let that unstable handle realignment?" Adia would have said, but Adia wasn't here, and Sael was. Let him prove himself now, especially working with Idosh. One test of discipline was the ability of an unstable to work in unison with someone who was stable.

Sael's eyes were wide as he stared at Jerik.

"Well? Why are you standing there? I told you to get with it!"

Sael shook himself from his daze. "Yes, sir!"

Jerik's attention was already on a new problem.

"Councillor, we've got minor burnouts on stations one, two, and seven on the bridge. Level eight is having trouble with an internal pressure rupture in the life-support system, down to fourteen percent operational with a flux to eight percent. Sections four through six of that level have been sealed off. Shipwide life support stands at seventy-nine percent. Engineering has two relief baffle plates out, and the hyperdrive fielder is partially disaligned. Repairs are expected to take fifteen kushas at the minimum."

Well, that was it, Jerik thought grimly as he looked out the viewscreen at the lonely expanse of silent stars. "So we're stranded in some future, perhaps thousands of years from our goal, with no knowledge of what kind of future we're in or what to expect from it," he said softly. "How have we shaped this future by not stopping the invaders from destroying Lym?"

He turned and walked toward the bridge doors. "I'll be in my quarters. Idosh, as soon as you get a compilation of facts on our whenabouts, pipe down the details so I can get to work on them."

Four kushas later Sael, finished at last with assisting the free-flight engineer, went to his small quarters to clean up and change. Then he walked down to the dining lounge, ordered a full meal from the ship's automat, and took it to a nearby table. There were few people in the lounge since it was not the normal dinner period, and he was content to eat in silence.

On the way out he dumped utensils and containers into the reconverter bin and decided to port back to his room. Although short distances did not affect him anymore, he became fatigued after using his powers to a great extent and had to wait until he was refreshed before trying them again. It didn't worry him, though; Jerik had explained that he would build up his tolerance level as he continued to exercise his powers.

Back in his room with little to do, Sael began pondering on the kind of future they were in. He pressed at his channels to see what might be there. A faint glimmer formed in his fix channel, and he grasped it, trying to stabilize it. As the scene developed, he felt apprehensive. Instinctively Sael tried to fight it before he realized he would have to let the scene unfold before him.

The land he saw was broken, unfamiliar, and marred with old fires and heavy artillery destruction. The bleak horizons stretched out, broken only by jagged outcroppings of black hills. A peculiar quiet about the region both fascinated and repulsed him, impelling him to find out where this desolate place was. Sael probed deeply into the channel and then went deeper still before he discovered, to his horror, that he was locked in it. Frantically he tried backing out. It was useless. All that could be done now was to follow the fix and port there, and he didn't want to do that because the picture was blurred. Fear and distance kept it wavering from view, and he could not see it with the precise clarity he knew was necessary before he could teleport. It felt terribly far away.

He called wildly to Jerik but received only silence in return. Terror pounded through him. Porting was the only way out, but with the distance and fuzziness of the fix, that would mean death!

Something stabbed through his channel, and a glimmer formed. An opening! Sael edged toward it. Blinding in its intensity, it leaped toward him.

"Now! Get out before it's too late!"

Mustering all his courage, Sael shoved himself at the light. Something caught him and yanked him through the opening. He opened his eyes and sighed as he saw his familiar quarters. Somehow he had made it out of the channel without teleporting, but the effort had been exhausting. He lay back on the bed.

"Sael?" Jerik's thought broke through. *"You made it okay?"*

"Uh-huh."

"Listen, don't do that again from this distance without help. You are too inexperienced."

The tone was not harsh, but Sael was suddenly angered by it. *"Well, you shouldn't have been prying around in my business!"*

"I wasn't prying around. You sent me that flash. There's a difference. If I hadn't given you the opening, you would have killed yourself. I'd like to see you in my quarters at kusha 2, and I don't want you porting in unexpectedly either."

The thought ended, leaving Sael resentful. He told himself he hadn't needed the proximate's assistance.

Nevertheless, at precisely a third point to kusha 2 Sael stood in front of the door to Jerik's room and sent a mental query inside. The proximate released the door lock, and the silver door slid open. Sael slipped through quietly and sat down in a chair. The proximate looked at him. Papers covered with figures were scattered about his desk, and the two small desk consoles showed various readouts. Jerik looked weary.

"I'm not disturbing you, am I, Councillor?"

Jerik smiled. "I wouldn't have asked you to come in here if you were going to disturb me."

"I'm sorry I got upset with you earlier. I tried to control my emotions, but I couldn't."

"I know." He shoved the papers aside and sat back in the chair. "It's not easy to keep your emotions suppressed when they react violently before you can think about what you're saying or doing. But you are controlling them well enough for what discipline training I've been able to give you. Now, why were you trying to port that far?"

"I wasn't trying to teleport. I got a fix. Then, when I tried to stabilize it, I got locked in the channel." He looked at Jerik a little anxiously.

"It takes practice to control your channels. That's why I gave you explicit instructions not to experiment when you're alone. You would never have made it to Galapix had you tried to port there."

"That's where my fix was?"

Jerik nodded.

"But it was horrible!"

"I know." The councilman's voice was quiet.

"What happened to it? How far in the future are we?"

"All I know about Galapix is what I've seen for myself, and that hasn't been much. I don't know what went wrong there. As far as I can tell, we are roughly 8,600 years ahead of our time. I don't know exactly."

"Can we get back?"

"We should. We just didn't know what to expect from the warp."

They both became quiet for a while, each with his own thoughts.

"Jerik?" Sael asked at last.

The proximate glanced at him.

"If we hadn't gotten caught in that energy band, we would have made it into the future you wanted, right?"

Jerik nodded. "We would be exactly 157.3372 years into the future from when we left our time. When Adia lost control of her board, though, the ship plowed into the warp out of control until we hit the brake sequence."

"But I don't understand."

"Understand what?"

"This future. It didn't exist in our time. How can we, 8,600 years from that time, exist now?"

The proximate was silent. He shrugged. "How does the time warp exist? How do we aim our ship, set course and speed, yet stay in the same place never moving save through time itself? I can't tell you, but here we are in this time. And what is time but a consideration, an altering of reality that allows matter, energy, and space to persist? Still, we have allowed this time, this future, to exist by not being in the past to prevent Lym from being destroyed. We exist now because we no longer existed in our time after we entered the warp." He smiled. "A paradox?" Jerik shoved his chair back and rose, walked around the desk, and leaned against it. "Space, Sael, is full of them."

His eyes pierced the young man's. "You've got your porting channel wide open to you, but you aren't in full control of it yet. However, aside from me, you are the only one on board who can teleport. I have to get to Galapix to see if I can find out exactly when we are. I don't dare try to bring the ship back into our time without knowing precisely how far in the future we are. We could be off in our calculations by hundreds of years."

"Why do you have to port there?" asked Sael, the mere thought of the wretched land causing him to shudder inwardly. "If there is information on when we are, can't you just get a fix on it from here?"

"No. I have to go there." He paused a moment, then added, "The area I want, though not porter-shielded, does not allow fixes on the information. The fact that the shielding turbulence still exists indicates there's a chance the data we need are there. And I want you to come with me."

"You know I can't teleport that far yet!"

"Maybe not, but I can. I'll link you through my channel, and you can port that way."

"I can what?"

"Teleport through a link with my channel. It's easy, as long as you have your own ability to port."

"How?"

"Here." Deftly he linked his mind with Sael's. The youth felt the connection snap shut and then felt Jerik direct him into his channel. Effortlessly he saw Jerik's precision fix on Galapix. It was different from the one he had had, and it was sharp and powerfully held in position.

"Just channel yourself right through. I'll help you along."

"Right now?"

"Yes. Now go!"

Hesitantly Sael began channeling himself toward the fix.

"Not like that! Go at it as though you really meant to port there. You've got half a sector to cross. You're not going to do it like that!"

Half a sector! Sael brought himself to an abrupt halt. He couldn't port that far! He tried to back out and realized that Jerik had purposely closed the channel on him. Now he had to port. He looked at the fix again: still clear and holding steady. Maybe he could make it. Sael braced himself and concentrated. Sudden blackness enfolded him. All semblance of balance and direction was lost. No, there, he had it again . . . there. . . . And he was on the ground.

They were standing at the base of a low, rocky hill. Here and there lay the crumbling rubble of ancient buildings, a few still vaguely similar to their former shapes. Tough grasses fought for a precious hold among blackened rocks, and beyond, tangled masses of trees grew to the edge of a vast charred wasteland that stretched to the horizon.

The area was unfamiliar to Sael. This was no part of Galapix that he had ever been to.

"Where are we?" he whispered. Wind whistled around the rocks, strengthening the feeling of utter desolation.

Instead of answering him, Jerik began climbing toward the great plateau at the summit of the low hill they were on.

Sael hurried to catch up with the councilman. "You know where we are!" he called out once as he stopped for a moment to catch his breath. He looked at the flat plains in the east. The sun, at its zenith, burned down on the razed world.

Jerik said nothing but continued his climb. Sael glanced up and hastened after him. The councilman's actions were mystifying. Sael reached out with his mind in hope of grasping some fleeting thought, and a surge of emotion struck him so poignantly that he almost staggered back. He told himself he wouldn't try that again and continued the climb.

At last he stood on the great plateau with Jerik. It was then that he realized it was not a natural surface. Polished and worn over the years, it was metallic, not stone. Sael suddenly knew where he was.

"The Council building," he whispered in awe, understanding the proximate's reactions, "from thousands of years ago . . . or where it stood."

The councillor merely nodded, looking out over the valley below.

Sael looked also. The surrounding land, rough and jagged, no longer resembled the rich green hills that had marked the picturesque setting of the magnificent building. Then he realized what had made the area so unfamiliar. He looked at Jerik.

"What kind of war could have been waged that would have annihilated the Laj Mountains and the other ranges around here?" The horizons were level save for four small ridges in the east, where in Sael's time there had been a tremendous mountain range.

The proximate only shook his head somberly. Sael did not dare press the subject further.

However, there was one question he could not hold back. "Are we the only ones left?"

Jerik didn't seem to hear him.

A worried expression on his face, Sael looked at the proximate. "Is there no one else?"

He received the sign of silence in return. Sael became quiet, afraid to say anything else, wondering what the councilman was seeing or sensing. He tried his own lines to see what answers they held; but they were unresponsive, and for once Sael did not feel like pressing them further. Giving up, he looked back at the councillor. Jerik stood there, his hand still half-raised as if he'd forgotten it, seemingly unaware of anything.

Suddenly Sael felt a searing emotion knife through him. In his mind, just for an instant, he thought he saw the proximate struck down by a strong blow. He looked at Jerik closely but could detect nothing in the silent, firm visage.

Many points passed before Jerik finally lowered his hand and shook his head. "No," he said with unusual softness in his voice, "we are not the only ones left."

"How many? Where are they?" Sael was unable to restrain himself any longer.

For the first time since they had come to the world, Jerik looked at Sael. No trace of the deep emotion he felt showed in his eyes or face. "We have our business still before us. Open your mind to me."

The abrupt shift in his manner caught Sael off guard, and the young man backed up a pace, unable to release his eyes from the proximate's deep gaze.

"Trust me. We are going to teleport."

As Sael opened his mind, Jerik took control and positioned him in his porting channel.

Well into the channel, Sael saw a richly decorated chamber lit by a single glowsphere. The room emanated great antiquity, secrecy, and power. Abruptly he and Jerik were in the room. He looked at the proximate, completely mystified.

"Where are we?"

Jerik tried to speak, but grief choked him. He turned away.

"Jerik, where are we?"

"In the Council building." His voice was barely audible even in the deathlike stillness of the room.

Sael stared at him. "That's impossible!"

"Oh?"

"We were standing on the main floor outside!"

Jerik turned back to look at him. His voice was steady, calm. "It had more than one level, you know."

"I know that—" Sael stopped, realizing he had thought

only of the floors that went up. But there weren't any levels that went down . . .

As if reading his thoughts, Jerik spoke softly. "There are many underground chambers in the Council building. Some of them have been destroyed by those who lived after our time, but they never reached the chambers of greatest importance."

More confused than ever, Sael asked, "What are you talking about?"

Jerik walked over to an old monitor and tried to switch it on. It was dead. Sighing, he turned back to Sael. "There are some chambers only the actual members of the Council and a very few others know about. This room is one of them. The chambers were built as part of the original complex long before our time, then their use died out. They were forgotten during the times of internal strife before the Interworld Council system was permanently established.

"During that time of strife movements to undermine the organization were started by some of the early council members. They had great powers and discovered these chambers and set up their operations here. The council members were not discovered until they had almost succeeded in disrupting the entire system.

"At this point there was a whole revitalization of both the Interworld Council and the building itself. The chambers were sealed off by special codes and powers and were forgotten by all but the members of the Interworld Council and those who the councillors decided might know about them. The changes in the system and the building brought about a stability in the entire system that lasted for 630 years, even until I was chosen to be a council member. And still the system survived, striving to accomplish the Plan: 'Worlds in unison through justice and wisdom.'"

His voice died off. He was lost in thoughts of the past, the glorious striving toward a broken dream.

Sael looked at him with renewed respect and awe.

Here, in this quiet room, the sense of authority emanating from the proximate deeply moved Sael. Light from the single glowsphere highlighted Jerik's windblown topaz hair, giving him a look as defiant as the wilds of space. The intricate Council symbol Jerik wore as a clasp at the collar of his silver uniform glinted in the light, capturing Sael's attention. The six green stones amid the silver weave of the medallion trapped the light with such brilliance that it kept Sael's eyes glued for some time. Only when Jerik shifted and broke from his reverie did the young man's gaze also break.

The councilman turned to a large case set on the floor and partially embedded in the wall. It was richly carved stone of gleaming green.

"What's that?"

"A history file directly related to the Council," Jerik said absently.

Sael let his eyes travel about the chamber. It was fairly large from what he could see in the light from the glowsphere. Several cases were set into the walls, all of the same green stone and all intricately carved with ancient symbols.

"What was this room used for?"

"A sort of storehouse of knowledge," was the response.

Sael looked at the councillor. He had knelt down to the stone case and was touching it lightly and in a peculiar way. The front hinged down in his hand. Curious, Sael went over to it. Jerik had pulled out a handful of flax papers and was seated on the floor beside the case.

"What's that?"

"Something you really have no business looking at."

"Oh." Sael was somewhat crestfallen, but Jerik paid him no heed. He was busy searching through the papers. He put a handful back and took out another.

"What are you looking for?"

"An answer to what happened to Galapix."

"We know that. The ones from the future destroyed the Council."

"No, we don't know. How was it destroyed? What happened then? What happened for the next 8,600 years?"

"But how are you going to find out? With the Council destroyed ..."

"This room hasn't been destroyed," Jerik murmured, shuffling through the bluish white papers. He stopped, looked at one of them, put the stack down, and began reading. "Here. This proves it."

"Proves what?" Sael glanced over Jerik's shoulder at the sheet.

"That the Council was not destroyed, at least not right away. After our disappearance Hedrick refrained from sending another ship out because he thought we were doing all we could in our future time, though he had no way of knowing for sure. By the time the attack was scheduled to hit he assumed something had gone wrong and had the city cleared. The black ship came, defeated the ships Hedrick sent out to destroy it, and attacked Lym. Not many were killed, but there was tremendous confusion afterward."

"How could one ship have defeated our—"

Jerik cut him short. "Kinetic experts. They manipulated our crews and kinetically guided their weaponry force against the ships and Lym. The Council building was not completely devastated, but it had to be extensively rebuilt.

"Hedrick died shortly after that. After my disappearance he had been ill-advised and the proximate he chose to follow him as first councillor led poorly. Hedrick did not have a chance to train him properly, and—" He stopped, and once again silence enclosed them like the walls of a tomb. The images on the papers before him blurred in a fog as he stopped reading to look at a memory.

"And? What happened?"

"That's when the disruption of the Interworld Council started," he said slowly, putting the papers back with equal slowness. "No one ever discovered who actually set it in motion, although various council members or their aides were suspected. It was also never discovered who made the assassination attempt on us. By the time the ship from the future was sent out to attack us in the past, thereby setting up the state of confusion, the people of that future were vicious. Those who could used their untrained powers to harm others." He paused again as if carrying a burden, the weight of which he had to shift before continuing. "They began to attack each other and became barbarians. That's when most of Galapix was finally destroyed. And that is where these sheets end."

"But if there wasn't a Council system, who recorded that? If only councillors knew about those records and these chambers ..."

"I said the system was disrupted, not destroyed. Until these sheets end, there was at least some semblance of the Council. There are other factors, too. Very few council members knew of these rooms. Only they knew of the information contained herein and ensured that the knowledge never fell into the wrong hands. When the last of those who knew about these chambers died, the history died with him."

"But we still haven't found out when we are! When do those papers end?"

"About 950 years after our disappearance." Jerik looked up at him.

"How are we going to find out when we are?" Sael sighed. "What we need is a chronocorder."

A ghost of a smile appeared on Jerik's face. "What made you think I didn't have that in mind in the first place?"

"You mean there might be one in operation somewhere?" asked Sael, astonished at the thought. "Here? In this desolate—"

"Maybe." Jerik cut him off, not wanting to be further reminded of the destruction of his world. He rose and headed toward the door, where he put his hand to a triangular pressure plate at its side. The door did not move. Frowning, he touched it several more times. "Can't be dead."

"Why don't you port out?"

"You can't always port down here." Abstractedly fingering the medallion on his collar, the proximate offered no further explanation.

"The porting turbulence?"

Jerik nodded, still looking at the door.

Sael turned away to look at the room again. He did not see the proximate remove his medallion and touch it against the door itself.

"Sael!" Jerik was standing in the open doorway when Sael turned.

"How'd you get it open?" He thought he saw the image of the symbol just fading off the door but decided it was a trick of the light.

"Persistence," said Jerik, vague testiness in his voice. "Come on. I doubt the door will stay open much longer."

Moist air struck Sael as he followed Jerik through the door. It smelled like a dark lake after sunset: cold but fresh. Jerik went ahead in the gloomy corridor.

"Where's the air coming from?" Sael's voice had dropped to a whisper in the muffled silence of the murky tunnel.

"Underground wind channels and caves, which are vented to the outside. It's a maze that's impossible to enter except through the Council building or by teleporting when the shields are down." He paused a moment, frowning. "The current was never that strong, though."

"You said there were others still around. Maybe they had something to do with that."

The councilman shook his head. "I doubt it. They're scattered in small bands over Galapix. I think it more likely time and artillery have taken their toll."

They moved on, their footsteps hushed in the dank darkness, the air chill.

"But what of the others?" Sael asked, needing the

comfort of Jerik's voice in the still tunnel. A blast of icy air hit him as they passed a branching passage. Somewhere down that way a rock fell. He jumped.

"I don't know," Jerik replied. "I do know they have lost their ability to telepath. Either that or they've developed it along lines that are unfamiliar to me."

They walked on. Sael groped cautiously. Jerik, traveling these black ways by memory alone, moved ahead slowly. They had been making their careful way for some time when they saw a dim light ahead. As they neared it, they realized the light came from a doorway that was open just a crack. Jerik stopped abruptly. Sael halted instantly at the proximate's action and was about to say something when a thought rammed into his head.

"Don't move. Don't say anything! Listen!"

Sael listened. His eyes opened wide. Muted voices were coming through the door. The words were unintelligible.

"Open your mind," said Jerik, *"carefully."*

Sael did so. At first he got vague and confused thoughts. Then, as he opened his mind wider, something powerful touched his awareness. He recoiled in shock. The voices had ceased. And now he was being probed by the minds on the other side of the door.

Chapter 10

SAEL SLAMMED HIS WALL up fast. Immediately Jerik caught his arm in a solid grasp. *"Steady."*

The touch calmed Sael a little. *"W-Who are they?"*

"We'll know soon enough."

They were silent as Jerik's disciplined mind reached out to those beyond the door. Slowly he released his grip on Sael, who guessed the councilman had been as startled as he at the initial mental impact. Sael looked nervously at Jerik.

"Brace yourself. They don't look like us."

As the door opened wider, Sael instinctively wanted to run but could not make himself move. He stood rigid, watching the door swing. Two figures stepped out. Squinting against the glare, Sael saw them clearly and was stunned. The two figures were hunched and frail. Thin, pale hair framed distorted faces crosshatched with fine lines. Large dark eyes looked out from drooping lids, giving their faces the appearance of having been forcibly pulled out of shape.

Jerik had been looking at them with intensity, ignoring their appearance. "It's all right, Sael," he said finally. "Open to them."

Not daring to disobey, the youth opened his mind. The first malformed man looked at him with startling suddenness. Sael tried to raise his wall, but it was too late. The thoughts entered his. The extreme gentleness of the contact surprised Sael. It was ethereal, not harsh as he had expected it to be, yet suggestive of great power and, oddly, full of eager curiosity. Curious himself now, Sael welcomed the contact. There was a long silence while each explored the other. At length the malformed man spoke, and the beauty of his voice matched the quality of his thoughts.

"We see you mean us no harm, and we mean you none. I admit you appear strange to us, but we will not allow that to stand in the way of making you welcome here. You above all, Proximate Jerik." He turned back to the room and motioned for them to follow. Sael looked at Jerik. The proximate nodded, and they followed the two bent figures.

The room was a large sitting chamber lit by a cluster of eight glowspheres. Along one wall, however, there was some very old equipment, some of which Sael recognized from his own time and some of which was unfamiliar. Two closed doors were on that wall, and on the wall directly opposite hung a heavy deep-green curtain concealing another doorway.

There were five other people in the room. Now that Sael could see them clearly, he was even more surprised. To him they were ugly, but their minds were cleaner and gentler than any he had ever come in contact with.

He didn't realize he had been staring until their guide looked questioningly at him. Flustered, Sael hastily averted his eyes, but not before the other quietly asked, "What is it?"

It was a long time before Sael, struggling to decide between truth and a polite lie, finally glanced back at him. "Were you all born looking like that?"

Jerik glared at Sael for the tactless remark, but the malformed man smiled. "I would ask you the same question. Were you born looking as you do?"

"I-I— Well, I . . . " Embarrassment flared up in Sael in a sudden burst of radiating warmth. He hadn't thought that perhaps he was ugly to them.

The man smiled again. "Don't let it worry you." He spread his arms toward the deep-set chairs. "Make yourselves at home." His sad eyes pierced Jerik's. "This is your home anyway, isn't it, Jerik?"

The proximate frowned.

"You are a council member is what I meant. This building, what's left of it now, was practically home to you, wasn't it?"

"You seem familiar enough with these chambers. Would you mind telling me . . ." Jerik began.

"I will. First make yourselves at ease here, though I hardly need to urge you." The malformed man smiled knowingly at Jerik, who didn't know whether to be annoyed or perplexed.

The two who had come to the door went to their chairs and sat with some difficulty. Sael thought that, once seated, they looked a little better and not quite so hunched, but he still felt uncomfortable observing them. As he and Jerik sat, the first man spoke again.

"I am Palox." He extended a crippled hand to the others one by one. "Ibal, Gamel, Doi, Seth, and, of course, my wife, Al-leah, and Ge-Nemn, my son."

The proximate nodded gravely. "It seems you know me well enough without introduction."

"And your companion Sael." Palox nodded. "We know. The history files show you were the first to penetrate the time warp, or so it was believed. You never returned to your own time or to any other time. We suspected it was your ship that broke the warp not long ago, but we weren't sure until you stood on the floor of the Council building outside."

"How do you know about Sael?" There had been no

mention of the young man in the history files Jerik had read.

"We have our ways." A blank look momentarily passed across Palox's face. Al-leah went behind a curtained doorway. Jerik watched her. He looked back at Palox, unable to read past the malformed man's blocks.

"Here, Jerik, we are the Council. No longer Interworld, perhaps, but nonetheless the Council of our people."

At that moment Al-leah stepped from behind the curtain, bearing a shimmering tray with nine intricately carved crystal-thin green-stone goblets. Palox took one of the gleaming goblets from his wife and regarded Jerik evenly.

Al-leah brought the tray around to Jerik and Sael, who accepted the drinks from her. Jerik became silent for a moment, fingering the delicate stone, his eyes on the ancient symbol carved amid the other designs.

"You aren't convinced, are you?" Palox smiled slightly. "I meant what I said. We are the Council here—in this time. We and our people live in underground caverns and occasionally above ground also. We seven govern what is left of them as best we can. The Council never really died. I grant you there have been many forms of governments: barbaric dictatorships, monarchies, even something resembling a Council group. For 200 years we lived under a sort of makeshift Council. Then about 50 years ago, when I was younger and more ambitious"— he smiled at the memory—"I began searching out the legends of the mighty Council that once governed this world. By sheer accident I came across these caverns, one of which had been breached by a bomb. I entered it and eventually found these rooms. As soon as I discovered the ancient information, I began a new Council. The system survives, though we no longer have contact with other planets. 'World in unison through justice and wisdom.' The Plan has been accomplished. We live in unison."

"The Plan accomplished?" Jerik said, bitterness edging

in his voice. "Is this what it meant? That our descendants would live in the shambles of what was once a beautiful world? The Council had been in effect 630 years before I became part of it. And in another 150 it would be destroyed. This is the result of that Plan. . . ."

The proximate could not mask his profound grief at the devastation of his people and their world, nor could Sael entirely blanket his own emotion.

"Do not fight what you feel. It is right for you to mourn the loss of something so precious," said Ibal, the other man who had come to the door with Palox.

Wondering what Ibal would know of fighting emotions, Jerik looked at him.

"We have learned emotions should not be fought," Ibal continued. "In our studies of your times we discovered that those of you who were unstable, as you called it, had the wrong idea about emotions. You seemed to think you had to fight and control them rigidly before you could begin to handle your abilities." Ibal smiled a little as if still trying to understand the reasoning behind this concept.

"Well, it isn't so. In fighting your emotions, you repressed them to the point of being unable to respond. All your efforts were expended in holding down those emotions. You became isolated from each other and your environment and, being isolated, became unable to reach out—mentally or physically—and thus, you lost your abilities.

"For what is telepathy but a reaching out to another, or teleportation but a reaching out to a place? Telekinesis, precognition—aren't these a reaching to an object or time? And isn't love a reaching out? Or excitement? Even negative emotions like hate and fear—they, too, are such.

"I have thought long about your people and their civilization and why it failed. It seems your primary error was in suppressing your emotions rather than understanding and handling them. So, of course, your original Plan failed. Yet the Council survived, albeit changed and adjusted to our needs. But we have peace."

Palox's voice was gentle. "Our people are scattered, but we are very close with our minds. Many of us still have abilities like teleportation and kinesis. You could not sense our telepathy because we use the different wavelengths that our ancestors developed to escape the mind probers of 6,500 years ago, approximately 2,000 years after your own time."

"You say that fighting emotions cost us our abilities, but nothing else can be done when they dictate our actions." Jerik felt as though he had reached an impasse. How could they possibly know what it was like to live one's entire life with emotions so volatile they could drive a man to kill with a single thought? No one stood a chance against an enraged, undisciplined unstable. All he had to do was recall Sael's reactions against himself, his own against Adia!

"Learn to deal with them, and accept them for what they are. It isn't wrong to feel grief and anger as long as you are the cause of them and do not become the effect of them. Your instability, as you called it, came about because you refused to allow yourselves to experience emotions. All you ever did was cover them up!" Palox seemed not to completely comprehend this. "Once we discovered emotions were not something to resist, we found we didn't have to worry about their governing our lives. When one is grieved about something, he is grieved, and we understand that. If he can express it freely, that is good. And equally good, he will feel joy infinitely more, express it, and be far happier than one who has suppressed his feelings."

"But when anger and hate run the better of you, what then? Emotions so vicious I don't think you could begin to understand their effects! You have abilities and are stable. You don't know what it is like to suddenly want to kill someone you know and to have nothing else in your thoughts!"

The pained look Palox gave him spoke more plainly than words. It took Jerik aback, and the brief concept the proximate received was of a time long past when people did simply that. "There are other ways of dealing with such emotions, Jerik. Bury them, and they'll only force their way out much more ferociously than if you confront and handle them."

Jerik wondered how he could do that and not let them get the better of him. Could Sael learn to deal with his emotions? Adia? Could any unstable fully handle his emotions without being overwhelmed by them first?

"There is still time," AI-leah said softly.

Jerik looked at her blankly. "Time?"

"Time to change. You weren't able to carry out your thoughts against her."

Something about her manner caught Jerik's attention. She had been reading him. . . . He felt the smoothness of her power touching him with ethereal lightness and realized she had been observing him quietly for some time. It was as if his thoughts had been exposed for her to read whatever she wanted. Yet somehow he knew it had been unintentional, as if she had accidentally touched upon his channels with her superior abilities.

"Accept it for what it is," she continued. "Go by your own wisdom whether or not an action is good. Handle what is not, and leave what is. That doesn't mean you will never hate, but you will find that negative emotions will lose their motivation."

"It is the only way you'll ever free yourselves of your violent impulses," said Ge-Nemn, "and be able to deal with your emotions without repressing them. Then the Plan will be accomplished," he said, as if it were the simplest thing anyone could do.

It was impossible to tell how old any of them were, and Sael wondered how old Ge-Nemn was. Although

Palox had mentioned finding the caverns fifty years prior, Ge-Nemn appeared to be as old as his father.

Sael was suddenly aware that Ge-Nemn was looking at him. Abruptly their minds met, and when Sael withdrew in awe of the simplicity and clean mental paths of the other, delighted to have found youthful eagerness there, he telepathed to him in surprise, *"Eighteen! You're a year and a half younger than I am, and you're a member of the Council!"*

Ge-Nemn tilted his head in a sort of shrug. *"Only because all agreed I fit the qualifications."* He grinned. *"Sometimes I'm not sure about that. They seem to know what they're doing when they choose, but I've heard say the ways of a councillor are as mysterious as they are many."*

Sael returned the smile good-naturedly. For the first time someone his own age accepted him and offered friendship.

Palox glanced at the two, and a smile formed on his wrinkled face. He turned back to Jerik. "It is not as difficult as you think," he said to the proximate.

In the silence that followed, Jerik thought back to his wanting to kill Adia the night before they plunged into the future. Always keeping his emotions guarded, he had not realized until that night what might happen if he could not hold them back. All unstables were like that, suppressing their feelings and never relaxing for fear of the consequences. Maybe that was not the answer, but how could he deal with them and not be overwhelmed in the process? He would have to think about that.

"Perhaps not," he said in belated response to Palox's statement. Then he looked directly at the man as if suddenly remembering his original purpose in heading for this room.

"Palox, we have to get back into the warp. 157 years from our own time a ship will ride the warp to destroy our capital. It sets conditions up for this future now. We have to stop it, and to do that we must know exactly when we are. Can you help us?"

The room became quiet. The seven had slipped into their special communication lines and conferred among themselves for several points. At last Palox directed his communication back to Jerik.

"The decision is difficult. Our society now is stable and secure. By going back in time, you will alter this era. We cannot foresee whether it will be worse or better. However, as a member of the Interworld Council of your own time you were known for your fairness and rightness of decision. Too, you must go back. You do not belong to this time.

"When you do what you must to alter your future, it may be that we and our time will remain the same on some kind of alternate time track. But we and our time may simply vanish—not be—having never existed. Or, and this is what we hope, we shall exist in your future, retaining the best of your times with the best of ours. Whatever will be, we will accept. Of course, we can prevent it by retaining you two, but we've all agreed this would not be best. Things are not optimum for us as they are. If you go back to your time, there is a chance we shall still exist, receiving much benefit from the change. It is a chance we are willing to take. Perhaps we shall know the ancient mountains and wildernesses that abounded with beauty. Our thoughts are our only gardens now—save for a very few untouched places on the planet."

Feeling Palox's wistfulness to experience a world he could only imagine, Jerik said, "You have shown me something today. Perhaps I can show you something before we leave. Will you join your thoughts with mine?"

They conferred and nodded in agreement. The proximate then looked at Sael. "You, too," he said, offering no further explanation.

The room grew quiet as the seven joined their clean, gentle thoughts with Jerik's. Sael also joined, wondering what Jerik intended to show them. He didn't wonder long. In his mind he saw the dark outline of a mountain range, the silver-pink of the early morning sky against the midnight-blue, the dim shapes of garden paths and trees. Awed, he became for the first time part of the morning sunrise, a sunrise of thousands of years before.

Chapter 11

THE OTHERS HAD WITHDRAWN their minds from Jerik's. They were lost, remembering the shimmering glory of the sun rising over lush wooded mountains in the simple quiet of early morning. Jerik, too, was lost, recalling his world, the people of his time, the Council with its idealistic Plan of government that had become a nightmare, and it reminded him once again of his task.

"Palox, can you tell me when we are? Is there a chronocorder still in operation here? Something we could use to pinpoint our exact location in time? We have to know before we venture back into the past."

Palox, still lost in the distant past, rose slowly. "Is this such a world as was once ours?"

"Yes."

"You must excuse us. We have never seen such a clear picture of the past before, what it was like to live when the world was alive. This was before you lost control of your emotions and became vicious."

For an instant Jerik thought Palox was referring to

him personally and then realized that was not so. "We have to get back. Can you help us?"

Palox turned to face him. "I can." He led them to one of the side doors, which he opened with a light touch to the triangular plate beside it. The room he showed them into held much equipment, including several medium-sized consoles. Jerik went to one and switched it on. The screen lit up, showing scattered lines and marks, and he worked with the keyboard until he was satisfied.

"How far have we come?" Sael pressed him.

"8,682.6970 years," Jerik said, but his eyes were distant, and his thoughts not on the subject.

"What is it, Councillor?" Palox asked quietly.

When Jerik looked at him again, he wore a sad smile. In his eyes emotion struggled for freedom, and some of that emotion was released. "To come this far into the future to find I can cry or laugh at my discretion . . . it is not something one learns easily. You will not be quickly forgotten, nor your Council here and now." He glanced back at the board and switched off the console. "I must get back with these data. Give the others our farewells."

Palox nodded formally. "Already I see you will open a new world for us. I extend farewells from all."

"What are we going to do?" asked Sael when they reached the ship.

"About what?" The councilman went behind his desk and sat down, mulling over papers still scattered about, appearing to have lost all interest in what had happened on the planet moments before.

"About getting back. About what they told us about our emotions. What are we going to do?"

Jerik had already buried himself in his calculations and seemed to forget Sael was still standing before him.

"Well?" Sael repeated.

"You're asking me to answer an awful lot right at this moment."

"But I want to know!"

"Give me time, will you? I have to get on this, or we won't make it back to our time. I suggest you get plenty of rest. We're going to have another rough day tomorrow. We'll be pulling out of this time as soon as repairs are effected, which should be sometime after midnight. Whatever you do, *don't* go plowing around your channels. Give them a chance to rest, too."

"Isn't there anything I can do?"

Jerik didn't even bother to look up. "Not now. Just get some sleep if you can. It will take the strain off your powers."

Sael left the room and walked along the corridor and down the lift to his quarters. There he lay on the bed and shut his eyes, letting his thoughts drift over the day's events and pondering on their next warp run with growing worry. Somehow weariness seeped into his troubled thoughts, and within a few more points he slipped into a deep, dreamless sleep.

The clamor of the ship's alarm woke him at 16 points to kusha 1. Sael shook his head to rid it of the remnants of sleep, and a thought hit him.

"All personnel stand by on full alert. We are attempting the time warp run again. We will ride this one out within the next two kushas or wait here for the next month for a stable entrance point into the warp.

"In this period there is a flux in the warp, rendering it highly unstable. We don't know what to expect regarding entry. All personnel are to assume their posts. Backup crews, prepare to man your stations. That is all."

Sael answered with the standard thought acknowledgment as he left his room. When he arrived on the bridge, the atmosphere was tense. Adia was not present, and Jerik was seated at her station.

"Free-flight engineer, lock onto navigation and give me your flight pattern readout."

"9.924.6."

Jerik moved two levers. "Scan and lock onto my board." He paused for a moment, then switched his monitor to the readouts of the other stations, rechecking them. "Good," he murmured. "Keep 'em clear, and don't let 'em slip. I don't care if it blows the ship apart."

Sael edged closed to him, his eyes on the monitor.

Jerik turned toward him. "I have to know if we're going to run up against any sudden accidents, as we did the first time through. Since I'm manning Adia's station, I am going to have to ride your perception. If you get a flash, I have to know about it immediately, especially its validity." He smiled. "You do seem to have a penchant for receiving flashes at opportune moments."

Sael nodded, pleased. He suddenly became aware of the precision with which Jerik had entered his mind and became aware also of the others on the bridge connected with him. He felt the linkup in wonder. It had never been quite like this in training in the academy. The concentration of the group intensified as they began the warp run.

The ship edged slowly into the warp, straining against entry. The outer hull shimmered in the brilliant blue of the energy band surrounding the time warp itself. The band bulged dangerously.

Sael caught a flash that the band would engulf the *Silver Nebula*, and Jerik, in connection with the young man, saw it, knew it was valid, and ordered the ship into reverse. The shuddering ceased, and they were back in normal space. The proximate sighed and leaned back in his seat, gazing out the central viewscreen at the battery of stars.

"Too fast, and it passes through us; too slow, and we can't break free," he said.

"We're going to have to risk its passing through the ship, Councillor," Idosh, the free-flight engineer, stated flatly. "The only way we're going to make it is to warp into hyperspace and warp from there into time."

Jerik sat back, still looking at the deep expanse of space.

"What if we went faster than our original entry speed?" asked Sael. "Could we avoid the energy completely?"

"The ship would buckle under the stress of that energy band," said Idosh. "The trial runs we made before should have told you that."

"I don't mean a top speed entry. . . ."

"We still couldn't do it," the engineer persisted. "That band's got a negative force-3 stress aside from the pull of the warp. We'd buckle—"

"Maybe not," Jerik broke in. "Not if we increased our speed no more than 2 marks."

"That wouldn't be enough," Idosh argued. "Even then we don't know if we can avoid its passing through the ship."

"It might be enough to lessen the chance of its striking someone. Idosh, set your board for an increase of 2 marks speed. Helm, I want a realignment of 416.6 degrees in conjunction with that speed." He turned back to his board, reset it, and gave the order to make the warp run.

The ship paralleled the warp, then increased speed and warped into hyperspace. The time warp lay open before them.

Sael saw the streak of blue leap toward the ship and knew the exact point where it would pierce the hull. It had to be stopped. Without warning, he broke away from Jerik's linkup. Suddenly feeling very much alone, Sael nevertheless concentrated on the channel in which he saw the energy. The channel was new to him; he didn't know how it should be controlled or what would happen, but determined, he forced against it. He saw the streak of blue pierce the hull and threw all remaining effort into the channel.

The channel suddenly split wide. And, incredibly, Sael deflected the blue energy into the ship's hull, where it streamed harmlessly away. The entire effort had taken only a short while, but it left him exhausted.

The ship ceased vibrating once they had passed through the energy band. Warped into the time track now, they headed smoothly and swiftly back into the era they wanted.

"*Well done.*" Jerik rejoined his thoughts with Sael's. "*Now let me back into your channel, will you?*"

Sael nodded shakily and opened his mind to the proximate.

"*How far back are we now?*" he heard someone ask the councilman.

"*5,110 years from our own time. Regression is going well. Helmsman, begin braking in 1,300 years.*"

The officer couldn't help wincing. "*Did you have to put it that way?*" he muttered. He had intended the thought only for himself, but Jerik as well as the others caught it through the linkup and chuckled.

"*Yes. Only make that 1,120 years now. Braking speed down 0.7 mark, easing to 0.003 mark on my command.*"

"*Right.*"

1,120 years were not as distant as they seemed. Only 4 points later Jerik's thoughts sliced through the linkup. "*Begin braking now.*"

Handling the ship was easy this time. The braking procedures went smoothly, and when they reached 0.003-mark speed, time was passing by in months instead of years. Suddenly Sael felt something vicious and wicked hit his mind. Shocked, he tried to erect his defenses, but something forced them down. He heard the others cry out. An instant later the ship jolted to a halt.

The proximate, too, had been caught by the mental trap. Control of his hands had been overtaken by a powerful kinesis. Rather than bring the *Silver Nebula* to a full halt in this era, he would have preferred to shove the controls back and take the ship to some distant time. But he had forgotten about the time riders.

Chapter 12

WHEN THE SHIP STOPPED, it slipped out of the warp into one of the most barbaric periods of the altered future: 540 years after their own time. Jerik and his crew quickly recovered from the initial attack and erected strong mental shields against the continuing barrages of fury and hate from the beings in the ships surrounding them. For a long time the silent battle raged, but Jerik and his crew held firm until the assaults finally weakened and stopped.

"Keep your guards up," Jerik warned urgently. "They will attack again if any of us relax."

"Who are they?" whispered Sael, shaken. "Where did they come from?"

"They're time riders. They were riding the future with their thoughts, caught us riding the time warp unaware, plunged in, and rode it with us," said Jerik. How could he have been stupid enough to ignore the reports in the history file? he asked himself. He should have known that the time riders of this era would intercept the *Silver*

Nebula. If his crew had not been so well disciplined, the time riders even now would have them all under kinetic control. Disgusted with himself, Jerik dropped his line of thought on the subject and opened a mental line to his crew under a guarded channel.

"They will attempt to probe us for information. Keep all but this line blocked and watch it closely. They must not learn any more about us than they know already. They are clever at slipping under blocks or bringing them down, so maintain a full barrier of confusion. Lidra Sconn and Itra Fenn, report to the bridge. That is all."

When the two women Jerik had summoned entered the bridge, the proximate turned to the fairer of the two and said, "Itra, I want you to lock in on them and see what you can uncover. Lidra" he addressed the other —"we'll need your kinesis later on. Balsk"—Jerik turned to his helmsman—"put a reversal screen in effect. If they're going to hit us with anything, they can just as well get it right back. And link up with Itra and see what you two can get."

Jerik moved to his command chair and turned his attention back to Lidra. "What are they capable of in telekinesis?"

The auburn-haired woman met the councillor's look with disquiet in her eyes. "They specialize in it. What I felt against me was malevolent and skillfully employed. Their evil intentions are powerful and unbridled."

"Can you slice their waves?"

"I don't know. I should be able to, Councillor, but I've never cut waves like those before."

Jerik remained silent for a third of a point, watching his crew member and sensing her trepidation. His eyes narrowed. "Do it!" he said bluntly, and turned back to the viewscreen and the menace of the three ships.

Under normal conditions, Jerik thought, three against one were not bad odds when you had a crew with a wide variety of abilities. But when the opponents you were facing had equally assorted powers coupled with a thousand percent increase in evil, the odds began to run slim for escape maneuvers.

"Councillor," his communications officer broke his train of thought, "they're signaling for ship-to-ship comm."

The officer's voice registered the same surprise that hit Jerik. Why did they bother with ship to ship instead of telepathy? "Put them through."

The voice that filled the bridge through the comm center was like metal grating across metal. "You are ordered to surrender to the Imperial Federated Council of Galapix. State your ship, home port, and ranking commander."

The belligerence of the statement made Jerik sick. He shook his head, taking a moment to compose himself to steel-hard control. "I am Jerik, proximate of the Interworld Council of Galapix, and I don't surrender to my own world."

"There is no Jerik, proximate of the Imperial Federated Council," came the rough voice. "We do not recognize you. You are to surrender immediately to the Imperial Federated Council of Galapix."

The proximate responded to the blunt command, matching tone for tone. "That is because we are not of your time. We are from your future." As if the dolts couldn't figure that one out, he thought. Apparently they weren't much on history. If they didn't recognize him as being from the past, he wasn't about to call it to their attention. For a point there was no communication from the other ship.

Itra Fenn broke the stony silence in Jerik's thoughts. *"They're trying to figure out how far in the future we come from. They can see approximately 410 years; for some reason they can't go any further. You don't exist in the time they know about."*

410 years hence must contain an enigmatic flux in the warp, Jerik thought, and then realized that the time period corresponded with the cessation of the reports in the Council's history files. Although the initial devastation of Lym in his era must have been great, Galapix's

planetwide destruction must not have occurred until that future time.

"*Itra, they don't seem very history-conscious if the name of a member of the Council doesn't have any effect on them. What about it?*"

"*As far as they're concerned, Councillor, they've conquered the past. To them we can't exist as someone from out of their past.*"

Jerik sank back in his chair, confident, as the metallic voice cut through the bridge again. "From exactly when in the future?"

"From a time you cannot see," Jerik answered, "and a time I cannot name to you. You would not comprehend it."

"You call yourself Proximate of the Interworld Council. Very well. It has been decided that you shall be taken to our Council before your ship will be allowed to pass back into the warp."

Annoyance passed over Jerik's face. "And if we don't agree?"

"You will be killed in the energy band of the time warp."

As simple as that, Jerik thought. It didn't pose much of an option, and he knew escape from their convoy was impossible under these conditions.

"*Itra, what about it? Are they bluffing?*"

"*They are not bluffing, Councillor. Utilizing their kinesis, and from other accounts I've been able to perceive, they are very capable of it.*"

The proximate mulled it over, then straightened in his chair and said quickly into the pickup, "We will go with you. Understand, it is only our personal curiosity that motivates us to take this action. I warn you, we have ways of overpowering you. We were caught once in your trap. We shall not be so caught a second time. Consider this communication closed."

Jerik motioned to his communications officer to shut the line, hoping he had sounded as threatening to them as they had to him. From a flash he had received, he knew he had thrown them into confusion simply by appearing to take charge of the situation. He became aware of the astonished stares of his bridge crew and glared back at them.

"Well? You heard me. We have to plot our course back into the warp so we can get back to the time we want without being pulled out again, and we're not going to do it here and now with them watching us and able to manipulate our ship. We're supposed to be from their future—and, speaking technically, we are—so we are supposed to be more advanced than they.

"Helm, don't let them drag us in with their tractors. Take the lead from them."

The proximate settled back in his chair, thinking. Powerful as these people's abilities were, they appeared to have lost the quality of wisdom in asserting their superiority. Jerik's taking charge of the situation would give them something to worry about while he figured his way out of the present dilemma. He would have to have some answer when he faced the first councillor—if there was one.

He slipped into a private line with Itra and Balsk, who had been working to find out what they could about the era they were in. The three conferred for a time, with Jerik casting a brief look in Sael's direction once and then continuing the discussion. After a while the councilman motioned to the young man, who looked at him curiously and came to where Jerik was seated.

"You showed some kinesis when we entered the warp from the future, didn't you?" The proximate's voice was quiet, almost thoughtful.

Sael nodded, feeling proud of the achievement but still curious.

"In fact, aside from me you have the widest range of powers on board this ship. Too bad you're not disciplined in using every one to its full extent."

"I'm learning quickly, sir."

"So I noticed. Now listen. You may need those powers before we get out of this because I am going to put you in one hell of a tight spot. You are going to be my son."

The words hit like a bombshell. "I'm what!"

Jerik grinned. "Don't think I'd do this for every unstable I happened to run into." He rose from his chair. "Balsk, keep a watch on things. I've got some planning to do with this kid. Sael"—he laid a hand on the young man's shoulder—"I think you would make an excellent son. . . ." They ported off the bridge to the proximate's quarters.

As soon as they were in the room, Sael released a barrage of questions, and Jerik motioned abruptly with his left hand.

"Just hold your silence and sit down. This will take a while to explain." They sat, and Jerik continued with hardly a pause. "We've landed in a nasty segment of our future, and from what I can determine, the Imperial Council wants me on Galapix to get information about the future they cannot see. They believe their distant future is much like their own time—only greater. They expect to reach the ultimate in power and glory, and they want that power and glory now. So there's not much we can do but play along and watch for any openings they leave us. I will have to go down there, and that's where you come in.

"In this time, as they assume will be the case in the future, councillors are very much in esteem if they have at least one son. Since I must go down there, I want you with me simply because of your range of abilities. I know you're not familiar with all of them yet, but we'll have to risk the consequences. If I get into a tight spot, I would feel more comfortable knowing your powers were with me, where they would be of some use. And the only way I can justify your being with me is by passing you off as my son."

"But what about my emotions? Suppose they come through?"

Jerik grinned. "That's the best part. They don't do much about controlling theirs. You just be your usual self, and you'll fit in." He clapped Sael on the shoulder to ease the insinuation.

"At this particular time, Sael, it's not so much that they care about their emotions, but they thrive on malice, greed, and other evils."

Sael didn't know whether to be shocked or disbelieving. Jerik looked at him with a sad smile. "It's a rotten role to give you, but if we are to get back to our time, we have to play the parts they expect us to play. Now let me brief you on the background information you'll need." With a swift thought transfer, Jerik gave Sael in a moment what it would have taken many points to explain with words.

Galapians used telepathy only for giving private orders or for probing minds, rarely for communicating, even over long distances. A person whose block was down could be torn apart mentally almost before he realized it. Their Council was structured differently from previous councils. Even the symbol and colors had been altered.

Jerik made sure Sael's mental blocks were strong enough to withstand whatever attacks he might encounter and showed him how to ensnare the network into a tighter wad of confusion.

"Okay," he said at last, "I think you're ready for them. Leave a private line open. I may have to channel my discipline through you if you have trouble with a channel you aren't familiar with. I have no kinesis channel, so I can't help you there.

"We're going to have to play this by intuition and guesswork. Leave your thoughts open for any hints on how you should act, but remember we are living a future that *could* happen, one out of many possible futures. It's a future we have to straighten out, not in this time, but by getting out of here safely and back into the past."

"I understand."

"Good." Jerik became silent. He received a private

communication from the bridge and then stood. "Back to the bridge while we achieve standard orbit. I understand their first councillor wants a few words with me."

They teleported to the bridge. Jerik quickly telepathed a few orders to the entire crew and then told his communications officer to open the line and put the conversation on shipwide.

A deep voice resounded throughout the bridge. "In salute to you, Jerik, proximate of the Interworld Council of the future, we welcome you to our time. I am Zarth, first councillor of Imperial Federated Council 58."

"I acknowledge your bid of welcome, but I want to know why, if you extend the welcome of the Council, my ship is under guard by your vessels," Jerik said.

"It will be under our watch until we make certain you intend us no harm."

"None intended, First Councillor. We are traveling time on a historical assignment."

"That explains your slow traveling speed then. You have instruments that record the situations of the galaxy while you are traveling through the time warp?"

"Our instruments are our own business." Jerik was curt. This man wanted information and would use brutal means to get it. "We wish only to get back into the warp. Our delay here is keeping us from accomplishing our mission."

"Very well. However, before we release your ship, I want to talk with you here in the Council building. The sooner we meet, the sooner you will leave and the better for all involved. I have much to discuss with you."

I wonder, thought Jerik, but all he said aloud was: "I accept your invitation."

"Your communications officer has the coordinates for transport."

"Of course," Jerik replied blandly. "My son will be with me."

"Your son? We had not made arrangements. I'm afraid—"

"It's perfectly all right. He accompanies me on all my time flights."

"He *is* your son, Councillor?"

"You would question my word?" Jerik sounded insulted.

"I question his admittance into highly private Council meetings."

"First Councillor"—the tone was deliberately overbearing—"in my time he is allowed into private Council meetings whenever I request his presence."

Sael wished it were true.

There was a long pause on the other end of the line. "A son of yours allowed into Council meetings?"

Judging from the tone of Zarth's voice, such a practice was unheard of, and its mere mention was suspicious. Jerik chose his next words carefully. "It is necessary in his case. He is proving to be very valuable to our Council. But must we discuss this over communications? I thought you wanted to see me in person."

"Yes . . . yes, I do. Bring your son. I will be expecting you."

Jerik made the gesture for cutting the communication line.

"Sael, are you ready?"

Sael nodded.

"Lock onto my channel."

Sael looked at the proximate, puzzled. "I thought he said we were to transport."

"I choose not to fall into that trap. Lock onto my channel."

In a few points they vanished from the bridge to appear in front of a large gray desk. First Councillor Zarth, a massive man in flowing red robes, sat behind it and looked startled, then displeased at their appearance.

"I hope this is enough of an indication of our superiority," said Jerik smoothly, noting Zarth's discomfort. "I wasn't about to be transported to a detainment cell.

I accepted your invitation to speak with you, not to be imprisoned."

"How did you know?"

"I read your mind," replied Jerik.

The first councillor turned a shade of ocher. "You read my mind!" Just as quickly, as it had surfaced the anger appeared to fade, and he smiled. "You caught me at a weak moment. That was very perceptive of you." The massive man looked at Sael, who stood beside Jerik.

"So this is your son, eh? He doesn't look like you."

"No," Jerik returned blandly. "He takes after his mother in appearance, but he inherits my abilities."

Zarth seemed to brighten at that and flashed a toothy smile at the young man. "He will have to demonstrate what he is capable of. But later for that. We have much to talk about. Come."

The time travelers were led into an adjoining room, which Jerik vaguely recognized as the grand meeting room; only it had been divided and arranged as a discussion chamber.

Zarth motioned toward a couple of heavy padded chairs for the two as he himself took a third and issued a telepathic order.

"I bid you relax and enjoy the comforts of our time, Proximate Jerik."

"Just Jerik. We don't normally call for stiff formalities in our Council."

Zarth smiled. "Nor do we. Call me Zarth. And your son? His name?" His eyes followed Sael's every move as the young man sat in the gold padded chair.

Repulsed by the man's attitude and expression, Sael was certain the first councillor was using every means available to break through his mental blocks. He lifted his eyes and swallowed his disgust. "Sael," he said quietly.

The first councillor started to say something and then turned when a door opened. Jerik and Sael, also turning, watched a woman enter the room. Her eyes were large and very dark. Long black hair fell loosely about her red gown. She carried a small tray that held three crystal glasses.

The tray was offered first to Zarth, who gave her a long look as he took one of the glasses.

"Do you approve of Azella? She's my primary." Zarth looked back at his guests.

"How could I not approve?"

Jerik sounded most convincing, Sael thought. For that matter, he was beginning to become convinced himself.

"Although," continued Jerik, "she wouldn't begin to compare with our women."

"Oh?" Zarth said, eyeing him carefully.

Jerik brought the conversation back where he wanted it. "I hope you realize we cannot stay in this time. We have to get back into the warp."

Azella extended the tray to the two time travelers. Jerik and Sael took the glasses and settled back in their chairs. Sael suddenly received a sharp thought from Jerik.

"Don't drink it!"

He tried to appear as though nothing had happened; but his hand trembled slightly with a quick surge of fear, and trying to take his mind off it, he glanced up at the first councillor's primary and found himself looking at her eyes—dark, hypnotic eyes. . . . He forced himself to look away.

Azella moved between Jerik and Zarth and sat on a floor cushion.

Jerik looked at her and then back at Zarth. "Do we have to talk around her, or is she going to leave?" he said bluntly.

"I told you she's my primary. She stays when I command her to stay."

Jerik shrugged. "As you wish."

"You really are interested in studying the time warp?" Zarth asked.

"Many of the early historical records were destroyed or falsified. We want to find out exactly what conditions were like during these times."

Zarth returned with the retort Jerik anticipated. "What better opportunity do you have to study them than to remain here? I insist you do."

"I didn't say the records of *this* time were destroyed. We have all the records we need of your great era. Anyway, we survey best from our ship as we travel through the warp."

"Your instruments are that precise?"

Jerik caught the suspicious edge in Zarth's voice. "Zarth, you are too eager for technology beyond your comprehension. What we are doing aboard our ship is of no concern to you."

The massive man shrugged. "Perhaps not. But you are perceptive. I had not expected that from you." He took a swig from his glass, finished it, and handed it back to the woman at his feet. "Azella, would you? And give our guests a refill, too." He noticed that neither Sael nor Jerik had touched his drink and motioned to them. "You'll find it vintage stock. The finest we have."

"I'm sure it is," retorted Jerik, his eyes fierce on Zarth. "We're simply not fond of drinking drugged yieri. I warned you about us, Zarth. We were willing to be polite—to a point. I want to leave now, and you are going to let me whether you like it or not."

Zarth seemed to shrink under Jerik's powerful glare. Then he regained his composure. His eyes flashed. Azella rose suddenly, the abrupt swirl of motion bringing Jerik's eyes in focus with hers. Sael leaned forward, caught by the woman's magnetism. Jerik, frozen to the back of his chair, was intent upon Azella. The moment lasted too long for Sael. It was her hypnotic effect, he realized, and he leaped out of his chair. "Jerik!"

At the same instant the councilman cried out in pain. The glass in his hand dropped to the floor. He slumped in the chair.

Sael reached out with his private line.

The proximate's thoughts were misty and confused. He struggled to overcome it. *"Injected . . . s-something in the back of . . . of the chair. Hidden trigger of some kind. I . . . I . . ."*

His mind had gone dark. Horrified, Sael stood staring at the proximate. Then he looked back at his own chair and saw nothing abnormal. Without another thought he whirled to face Zarth, his emotions roaring to life. "You vile slime-devil!" The untouched glass in his hand was flung at the massive man. It froze in midair and flashed back at Sael, crashing against his boots.

"Consider yourself fortunate I didn't wrap that around your throat, half-wit! Powers," he said with a sneer. "You talk big, but you're nothing. Nothing! Your father, sitting there with his display of wrath, didn't know what was coming."

Zarth had risen and now towered over the young man, who refused to back down. "Councilmen you call yourselves. We'll see about that. You're under our control now. And you won't escape us, half-wit. Not until your mind has been pried into and your channels have been ripped apart. You won't have any particle of thought left untouched. It will all be destroyed when we get through with you. You'll be stripped! Mentally stripped clean!" His voice reached the mighty walls and reverberated in Sael's mind.

You'll be stripped! Mentally stripped clean!

Chapter 13

FOR A WHILE SAEL stood, petrified by the threat. Suddenly the young man's rage erupted. "You're nothing more than rotted filth. . . ." he screamed.

The words ended in a strangled cry. Something pulled at his throat, choking him. He struggled against Zarth's kinesis, tightening like a noose around his neck.

Sael's savage fury and raw force crashed against Zarth's. Unprepared for the sudden attack from the young man, Zarth lost control for a split moment. Grasping the chance, Sael ported to the other side of the room. Zarth, in his rage, did not notice Sael's abrupt disappearance, and the channeled kinesis intended for Sael smashed against a chair, shattering it.

Seeing that Sael had vanished, Zarth whirled around like a crazed animal searching for its escaped prey. Mentally he summoned six guards.

Meanwhile, Sael strained to get a fix on the *Silver Nebula*. In his somewhat weakened state it was difficult to hold the picture steady. It was taking too long. The door opened, and six guards in gray uniforms advanced, circling him. He saw they were unarmed and wondered if their mental abilities made weapons superfluous.

Still trying to get a fix on the ship and playing for time, he shoved a few insolent thoughts at them and ported to the other side of the room. They were surprised, and he realized teleportation had not been expected of him. Zarth, Sael remembered, had already underestimated him, and that might give him the edge. Watching the guards move warily toward him again, Sael realized that teleportation was an unfamiliar practice in this time.

His fix finally stabilized on the *Silver Nebula*. He knew he should leave fast, but he couldn't resist shoving a last thought at Zarth. That almost cost him his life. Even as he began to port, tremendous pressures were exerted against him, hammering like solid blows to his chest and making him lose control.

Doggedly he fought against the pressures, and focusing full determination on the *Silver Nebula*, Sael began to overcome the opposing forces. Slowly the margin widened. The pull against him weakened, and suddenly he was overshooting his mark in reaction. His fix wavered, and steadying it proved almost more than he could handle.

As his body stabilized in the normal universe, his legs buckled, and he fell to the bridge floor, conscious but shaky.

Someone stooped beside him. Sael attempted to sit up and was carefully assisted. His vision cleared, and he noticed who had helped him.

"Councillor Adia!" For a moment he forgot his pain. "I-I thought you were still out from your accident," he stammered.

"Not anymore, I'm not," she replied.

Sael tried to ignore the pain in his chest. "Jerik's been

drugged a-and . . ." His mind was still in a whirl from the strain of porting and the kinetic blows he had received from the guards.

"We know." Her dark eyes pierced his, reminding him of Azella and her strange hypnotic power. He glanced away.

Councillor Adia let him sit on the base step of the bridge pad, giving him a chance to ease the tension in his mind and loosen the pain in his chest while she spoke to him.

"Because of the private channel we're on, we didn't catch what was happening down there until Jerik sent a dispersed thought saying he'd been hit with some kind of drug. We tried to lock onto both of you with the transport, but the entire city is shielded from that tighter than a vacuum lock in a shuttle. When I finally got my attention on you, you were having problems with that overstuffed slime-devil who calls himself first councillor.

"The important thing now is to get Jerik back, and there's nothing short of porting that can do that. You are going to have to go back there and find a way to get him back to the ship."

"I don't know if I can make it down there again. My powers are strained." Sael didn't want to sound negative, especially to her, but he was worn out.

She looked at him evenly. "You'll do it. They're not that strained. Powers have an amazing capacity for rough use before they reach their limits."

Unaware of the risk he was taking by straining his not fully disciplined powers, Sael merely nodded compliance.

"I sense where he's been taken," she said. "Lock onto my channel, and get your fix from it."

Despite his weariness, Sael found it easy to get his fix from her, and he backed out, preparing himself for the long-distance teleport.

Wordlessly Councillor Adia stabilized him so the fix

would not waver. Tense, nervous, he felt her steady thoughts and then with determination plunged into his channel.

Sael found himself in a small room lit only by a dim yellow glowsphere. Jerik lay on a richly decorated bed. Heavy maroon curtains concealed much of the wall space, giving the room a musty ambiance. Sael was about to go to the proximate when he received a flash that someone was approaching the room. After glancing about for a place to hide, he quickly moved behind a portion of the drapes. He peered out cautiously as the door opened.

Zarth's primary, Azella, moved in through the door and shut it behind her. Jerik stirred on the bed and opened his eyes. He felt disoriented. A woman was talking to him, but he couldn't see her clearly.

"You'll be all right, Jerik. It just takes time for that stuff to wear off."

As Jerik's vision cleared, he sat up, focused on Azella, and became trapped by her dark, hypnotic eyes. He sensed things were not quite right but couldn't shake her look.

"Don't fight me. Don't fight your thoughts."

Something stirred in the dim halls of his mind. Fight! That was it! He had to clear his mind, rid himself of the sticky swirls of murk induced by the drug and her hypnosis, but weakened, he slipped helplessly to her will.

From behind the drape, seeing the proximate succumb to Azella's force, Sael frantically searched for some channel with which he could help Jerik. He found something and channeled all his intention into the councillor's thoughts.

"Jerik!"

Sael could not tell whether Jerik heard him. He called out again and was relieved when the proximate responded. But it was not the response Sael expected.

Black ridges of blind, vindictive hate were thrust at him. Sael stood his ground. *"Resist her, Jerik! Fight her! Get rid of her!"*

Responding only to Azella, Jerik knew that something ugly and unwanted was intruding. He attacked it, forcing it away. Yet there was something vaguely recognizable about the intruder.

"Jerik!"

The tone of the command seemed familiar, but he could not place it.

"You've got to listen to me! Get her out of your mind! Fight her!"

Fight? Get her out of his mind? Listen to . . . whom? Then Sael's words made sense. Jerik suddenly understood the warning. He turned on Azella, trying to push her out, but she was overpowering.

Again he felt Sael reach out to him. Jerik drew strength from the young man, using it to fight the woman's opposing will. Slowly Jerik gained control, growing more aware of his surroundings and of Azella, who was standing by the bed.

Jerik rose and grabbed her arms. She looked at him, startled, then returned to her hypnotic gaze. "You're hurting me, Jerik. You shouldn't do that."

He avoided direct eye contact and tightened his grip on her arms. "If you were in my time, you'd feel pain worse than this! Get out of here before I really hurt you!"

"Not before you tell me what I want to know."

The statement was a trigger. Jerik felt foggy again, as if she were blanketing all other thoughts. As his will sagged, his clenched fingers relaxed, and with a swift movement her arms were free.

Sael channeled more of his strength to the councillor. Again Jerik took it willingly, fed on it, grew with it. Azella's mesmeric hold was broken again, and this time the proximate was determined not to let her regain it.

His fingers dug mercilessly into her soft skin. "I told you to get out of here."

"Not before you tell me what I want to know."

They locked in a battle of wills, with Jerik drawing strength from Sael. Together they forced the woman back and shoved their power deep into her mind. Terrified, she screamed and bolted out the door.

Jerik went back to the bed, sat down, and straightened his tunic, still enraged at the woman and at his own stupidity for getting caught in the trap.

"Jerik!" Sael had to call three times before the councilman looked at him, and the youth froze at the anger in his eyes.

The proximate suddenly recognized Sael and dropped his fierce glare. "Sael!" Then he cast him a sharp look. "Were you behind that curtain all that time?" Channels muddled, Jerik hadn't been able to place where the young man had been.

"Yes, sir. I ported here, and then Azella came in, so I hid back there."

Jerik smiled and rose and laid a hand on Sael's shoulder. "Thanks. I should have known better than to leave myself vulnerable to her power. Let's get out of here."

The councilman tried to get a fix on the *Silver Nebula* and couldn't. The drug was still affecting his mind, clouding up his channels. "How long is this stuff going to last?" he muttered.

"Can't you get a fix on the ship?"

"Not with this drug dulling me. Let me try through you."

Sael opened his mind to Jerik. Dimly he got a fix on the ship, but something was wrong. He couldn't orient himself to the channel as he had done before. Jerik tried to align him with the channel, but while he was befogged by the drug, it was useless. "I can't help you. You just have not done enough long-distance porting to get the fixes with the proper clarity whenever you want them."

"But I did it twice a few points ago."

"I know," Jerik sighed. "But you don't have enough control yet to do it all the time. You've also strained your channel, and you're just going to have to let it rest before you attempt great distances again."

"What about short distances?"

Jerik shrugged. "I don't know. It's your power. I wouldn't suggest using it for a while. Give it a chance to rest before you strain it beyond your control and wind up in infinity."

"Then it looks as if we're stuck here. Councillor Adia told me they can't get through with the transport."

"She's back on the bridge, hm? I was too busy with Zarth to keep any attention on the ship. Well, I figured she'd be in the middle of things before long. Can't keep her down. Transport's out. Well, that fits, too," he mused, half to himself. "At least I won't have to worry about that."

Sael looked puzzled. "What do you mean?"

Jerik glanced at him. "Transporters used to disorient me pretty badly, and when I got into porting, it became even worse. Even Raien can't figure that one out, and he's the leading orientationist on Galapix."

"Then you can't transport at all?"

"I can do it, but I disorientate." Jerik shrugged it off. "But if I had my choice between that and staying here, I'd be willing to be disoriented for half a day."

Sael stiffened suddenly. Alerted, Jerik slipped into silent observation of what the young man was seeing. Sael willingly let him watch. First Councillor Zarth was heading toward their room, and two guards were following him. They were still on the central floor of the building, but their destination was already clear to Jerik and Sael.

"Think you can port outside the building?" Jerik

wanted to take no chances on meeting Zarth face to face again if he could help it.

"What about you?"

"Don't worry about me. Can you port outside the building?"

Sael tried to get a fix and found one. It was stable enough. "Yes."

"Go ahead and keep your line open. I'm going to try to ride it since my own porting is out."

Sael nodded. He plotted himself on the fix and suddenly was outside in the deep fields in the foothills of the Laj Mountains, which had not yet been leveled as they had been in Palox's era. He felt Jerik lock onto his channel and concentrated on keeping the line open. As Jerik started to come through, Sael winced. The pressure became overwhelming, and his sense of balance slipped on him. The channel snapped shut.

"I can't do it!"

"I know. You're just not disciplined enough. Come on back; I'll need you here more than in some stray field."

Sael reappeared a short while later. "I had trouble getting a fix on the room."

"It's giving out on you, huh?"

They sat on the edge of the bed, looking at each other. Sael glanced away and nodded.

"How about your other channels? Are they doing all right?"

"I guess so."

"Just relax. They won't get here for another 2 points anyway."

The room was silent for a short while. Then Sael spoke again. "What about the rest of your channels?"

Jerik shook his head. "They're all out."

"Before, when you were fighting off Azella, we blended our powers. Do you think we can do that again? Maybe with your discipline to strengthen my channel, we can port to the ship or, if not, at least get out of here."

Jerik smiled. "It's worth trying."

They prepared themselves. Their minds met, opened wide, and became entwined. "I think I've got a fix on the *Silver Nebula*," said Sael.

"Keep with it. I'll see if I can lock us onto it."

For a moment there was deathly silence in the room. And then without warning, the door flew open.

Chapter 14

JERIK AND SAEL TURNED simultaneously and found themselves facing Zarth and two guards holding antem rods. The clear, slender weapons were leveled at the two time travelers. Jerik wasted no time. He shoved Sael into his kinesis channel.

The rods streaked with lavender brilliance. Sael strained to keep the lethal rays from reaching them. They were kinetically controlled and fought to dodge his power. Twice they slipped to the fringe of his force. Sael managed to block them, but exhaustion worked against him. His power flashed in uncontrollable spurts of violently fluctuating energy. One spurt crashed against the lavender beams with such ferocity the rays slapped back against the guards, killing them.

Infuriated, Zarth attacked Sael and Jerik with his powerful kinesis. Sael confronted the first councillor with awesome force.

Suddenly a thought occurred to Jerik, and the proximate branched out on a private line to the ship. *"Adia! Find*

Zarth's telekinetic wavelength, and sever it! If you can't, channel your kinesis through Sael!"

Abruptly Zarth found himself fighting a third force. Unprepared, he withdrew his attention from the two time travelers. Diverted by Adia, Zarth was hit by a massive surge of power from Sael, knocked off his feet, and was unconscious before he hit the floor.

"Adia, I can't port, and Sael's too weak to help me. We'll have to transport if you can find the source of that shield over the city."

"No good. We've tried to locate it. They've got thought scramblers set up all over the city. You're going to have to go on your own down there. What's wrong? Drug completely affected your channels?"

"All of them. Is the Silver Nebula *still under guard?"*

Jerik and Sael stepped over Zarth's body and moved cautiously into the quiet corridor.

"We've got one ship hovering beside us that's not about to let us out of its gunnery range. They've already tried to stick their tractors on us and got a taste of our defense. They're just watching now."

"Get everything set up for the warp run. Follow my last calculations to determine our entry and control of braking for 383.112 years past."

"Do you intend to hit it full speed?"

"If we have to. Your kinesis and Lidra's should be more than enough to shove that energy band out of the way to allow us free access at any angle."

"383 years isn't much of a margin at that speed."

"No. We can't afford to overshoot the time line. Just get the ship ready. We'll move out when I get back on board."

Jerik ended the communication, and he and Sael walked along the corridor and into another hallway. The proximate seemed to know his way fairly well, but many turns were new to him. They went on for some time before he finally stopped and leaned against a wall, glancing back the way they had come. The corridor was empty.

"We'll never make it out this way," he said in a low voice. "Snoop around with your channels and see if you can find a way underground. The way this place has been rebuilt, I don't know what they've got."

Sael was quiet for a while. Then he said, "I've got a mental picture of the inside of some room, a small office, I think. But that doesn't seem to have anything to do with the underground chambers. It's on the main floor."

Jerik nodded knowingly. "Where are we in relation to that room?"

"The second floor diagonally across from it."

"I thought we were on the fourth level," Jerik muttered. "Listen, you lead from here on. I don't dare trust my senses with this drug still fogging them up."

They wound their way around two more halls, alert to forewarnings of approaching danger. At length they reached a lift, which they took to the main floor. From there they had to cross the main entrance hall.

The hall was relatively quiet, as the rest of the building had been. The few men they passed gave them curious stares, but nothing beyond that. This area had not been rebuilt to any great extent, and Jerik moved confidently to the office. As they entered its vacant outer chamber, he asked Sael if the inner chamber was occupied.

Sael checked mentally, shook his head, and they went for the door. The councillor reached out and touched its silver surface lightly. It refused to open for him, and he pulled his hand away slowly, thoughtfully. "Sael . . ." he started to say, but Sael interrupted urgently.

"Someone's coming! A member of the Council!"

The drug still bothered the proximate. He felt slightly disoriented, and his head felt like swamp mud. There was no way he could port, and he would not allow Sael to overwork his power, strained to the limit as it was. There was no alternative. They would have to face the man.

A moment later a red-robed figure entered the outer office. A hard-eyed, dark-skinned man, he halted on seeing the two intruders and then leveled an antem rod at them.

Jerik faced him. "I am Jerik, proximate of the Interworld Council of the future. We need this room and have Zarth's agreement to use it."

"He's not told me of any agreement made with you, future man," the councillor said roughly. "Move from that door!"

Jerik stood his ground. "I don't doubt that Zarth has been too preoccupied with his primary to have told you anything. You'll find the authorization correctly given, but I doubt you can reach him now for verification."

The dark man was silent for a moment, trying to reach the first councillor mentally, and then he focused his attention on Jerik. "I can't contact him. But that does not stay my suspicions of you. I'll find out soon enough if what you say is true. I can wait."

Jerik relaxed slightly. As he suspected, if a mind was unavailable, it was assumed that the person was not to be interrupted. The development of power for selfish gain, and the disregard for emotional response the people had, had blunted their telepathic abilities.

"Since when does a member of the Council ride out suspicions and bypass the strict trust entitled to each and every member? I may be from a different time, but I am a council member nonetheless. Or doesn't the Council of this time treat its members accordingly?"

The red-clad man pointed his antem rod at Sael. "He is no council member. For that matter, you do not have the proper symbol of the Imperial Federated Council."

"We're from a different time! Don't you think after several hundred years or even several thousand the symbol's bound to change? Hasn't it changed from what it was in the past?"

The hard eyes of the other councilman narrowed suddenly. Horrified, the proximate realized his mistake and berated himself once again for the befuddled state of his mind.

The antem rod shifted back to Jerik, but the councilman never had a chance to use it. In a burst of fury Sael blew out of control. Throwing all remaining mental power into his channels, he lashed out at the red-robed councilman. The force rushed out uncontrollably, and the man stiffened and fell to the floor.

For a time Sael stood stunned before weakness overtook him, and he swayed and staggered back against the inner office door. He closed his eyes tightly, feeling drained.

Jerik went to the fallen man and took the antem rod. Scrutinizing the weapon in his hand, he turned back to the closed door.

Sael opened his eyes to find Jerik fingering the touch control in the handle of the rod. "Will he be coming around soon?"

"Hold your silence. They'll all be coming around soon. He got a signal out to the guards before you killed him." The proximate straightened. "Get back from that door," he commanded.

Sael watched him in a daze. "I . . . what?"

"Get away from that door!" He took Sael's arm and pulled him back. "Don't think about what just happened. Once that door is open, follow me through and don't stop to look around. Get the idea?" he snapped.

The authority in Jerik's voice jolted Sael. "Yes, sir!" he said automatically.

The proximate extended the rod, touched the buttons, and a lavender beam laced out to encompass the entire door. A moment later the beam ceased, and the door remained perfectly intact.

"Nothing happened!" said Sael.

Jerik moved quickly to the door and touched it again. This time it opened without delay, and he was through.

Sael lost no time following the councillor into the inner office. The door slid shut behind them. Jerik was already at the far wall. His Council symbol was off his collar and in his hand. The green stones in its silver center glowed with unnatural brilliance.

Sensing the volatile energy it emitted, Sael instinctively backed away.

"Follow close behind me," said Jerik. "The door won't stay open long."

The councillor touched his symbol to the wall, and fascination overcame Sael's fear as the wall instantly took on a glow of its own. As Jerik pulled the medallion away, the area it had touched assumed the color and shape of the symbol. Then it flared up brightly, and the entire wall panel slid open.

"Move!" The thought knifed into Sael's mind. He hastened close behind the proximate, and as the panel snapped shut behind them he got a flash of guards entering the outer room to see nothing but the dead councilman. Sael glanced about. They were in a small cubicle bathed with soft light from the floor panels. The walls were bare, and nothing was fixed to the ceiling.

Jerik pressed his symbol to a side wall. When he removed it, the wall flared brilliantly, and the cubicle they were in plummeted abruptly.

Sael's stomach lurched. Jerik stood perfectly still but looked abstracted, as if he were searching for something.

As his features relaxed slightly, the lift stopped. The side panel slid open. Jerik moved out quickly, and Sael, still unbalanced, somehow made his way out, stumbling into the corridor before the panel snapped shut.

Jerik turned and grasped his arms to keep him from falling. "Steady." His gray eyes met Sael's, and the young man felt a calming mental flow wash over him; it eased the nausea and gave him strength. He looked at the proximate gratefully.

"Are these the same chambers we were in in the future?"

Jerik nodded. "Let's go someplace where we can rest for a while."

The air was cool, not dank, as it had been in the far future, nor was there any breeze, but it was fresh. Jerik walked with complete confidence along the now-lit corridor, and Sael hurried to keep up with him. Then the proximate stopped and tried one of the slick silver doors along the way. It refused to yield to him. He took his medallion out again and pressed it against the surface. The same phenomenon occurred, and the door swung inward.

Sael recognized the vacant room as the one they had occupied with Palox and the others. He almost expected the hideous-looking people to be there, but of course, they weren't. The room was set up differently, more like a conference chamber than a lounge, but it still had deep-set chairs and comfortable surroundings.

Once they were in and the door shut behind them, Jerik turned and pressed his symbol to the door again. This time, as the wall blazed, nothing happened.

Sael eyed him curiously. "What are you doing?"

"Locking it and creating a porting turbulence so no one can port in here, or transport, for that matter, even if they know where we are. We can't port, either, unless I release the lock."

Satisfied they were out of Zarth's reach at last, Jerik ambled toward the curtained doorway, while Sael sank wearily in one of the chairs. As the councillor disappeared behind the thick drapes, Sael called out, "What's back there?"

"A wine cellar."

The proximate returned shortly with two green-stone glasses and offered one to him. Sael recognized the glasses as those that existed in the far future but was reluctant to take a drink after what had happened earlier.

Jerik grinned. "Look, I know this stuff's okay. Go on, take it." He sampled the beverage and indicated that Sael try it too.

Sael tasted the drink. It was satisfying as well as refreshing. He relaxed in the silence of the room, savoring both the quiet and the drink, watching Jerik, who was immersed in his own thoughts. He noticed the Council medallion was back on Jerik's collar. It had lost its glitter and appeared quite ordinary, as if no special power were connected with it.

"Do all glowstones react that way?" Sael asked at length.

"Mmm? What way?" Jerik was drowsy from the effects of the drug, the drink, and the comfortable chair.

"How it acted when you touched it to the walls."

Jerik shook his head. "Depends. All glowstones react to certain chemical or electrical stimuli. Here in the Council building certain walls were specially treated with chemicals that excite and react with the inherent power of the stone. The symbol was formed into the wall chemically so it acts as a key. When this"—he held out the medallion—"is applied with correct pressure and form, the mechanisms in the wall respond accordingly. That's why the people of this time haven't been able to ruin this place down here, because they've changed the symbol. Even if they did suspect hidden walls or special locks, they couldn't make them work. This is the only key."

He fingered the symbol, which was slightly smaller than his palm. It was impossible to tell what his thoughts were as he touched it.

Sael grew quiet. The memory of what he had done in the room above hung like frayed cobwebs in his mind. "I feel completely drained," he murmured, trying to finish the rich liquid in his glass and catching himself starting to doze. He shook his head to rid himself of the sleepiness.

"Using your powers when you've never had any firm control over them puts a lot of pressure and strain on you. That's why you killed that councillor instead of rendering him unconscious or giving him a nasty headache," Jerik said, knowing what was on Sael's mind. "You had no control over your channels. It was either all out or nothing. You couldn't have controlled it at that stage if you had tried. That's what drained you, releasing everything at once like that."

"But I didn't know I could kill him . . . or anyone! I've heard of things like that happening, but I didn't think—" His voice broke off.

"That it could happen?" Jerik finished for him. "That you were capable of it? You let your powers get out of control." He leaned back languidly, shutting his eyes. "Don't let it worry you."

Sael stared at him in disbelief. "But I—"

Jerik sighed and opened his eyes. "Sael, what do you want me to do about it? Hold a court session right now because you inadvertently killed someone in self-defense? Let things rest. Had you let yourself get out of control that violently in your own time, for no reason, you would have been placed under heavy restraints in a control center. But with this future's not being real anyway, let it serve as a warning of just what is possible with your force."

"What do you mean, this future isn't real? What about the drug you received? The kinetic blows I got from Zarth? I felt those blows. That drug's still affecting you. What about this room? These chairs? This drink?"

"I didn't mean physically not real," Jerik said. "This future is as real as any, as real as Palox's time, because we have let it happen. We weren't around to stop the ship that destroyed Lym 450 years ago. We were traveling in the time warp at that point and bypassed it completely and were well into the future. So the attack came right on schedule, as it did in the premonition. That set things up for this future. Think what would have happened if we'd been there to prevent that ship from leaving its time and going into the warp to destroy Lym. Think! This future would be totally different. There wouldn't be any Zarth or Azella or drug fogging up my channels. The Council would consist of different people, and the buildings left as intact as in our time. Perhaps.

That's one of many possible choices. When we do get back to our time and things are straightened out, we have to insure that such a thing won't happen again. We have to follow what Palox told us: Don't bury our emotions. Deal with them or experience them so we can ensure our future will not be corrupt as it is now."

Jerik rose and glanced at Sael's empty glass. "Want some more?"

Sael nodded.

Jerik took the glass from his hand and went back behind the curtained doorway, emerging a point later with the glasses filled; this time with a dark, thick liquid.

Sael examined the drink. "What's this stuff?"

"Edri-pasip. It's a protein complex. I'm afraid it will have to serve as food for now. It'll last you the night, though."

Sael looked at him quizzically, realizing for the first time that the proximate had no intention of leaving.

Jerik caught the look. "We're staying here until your channels are rested, and we'll see by then if this drug hasn't worn out of my channels. It should after I get some sleep." He put the glass to his mouth and drank. "This should move it along, too." He sat down and glanced at Sael.

Sael looked exhausted and worried. Jerik recalled his first impression of the young man in the corridor in the space center. He had sensed Sael's undisciplined power, although he brushed it off at the time. Being forced to handle undreamed-of situations in an insane future, however, was a strange way to discipline those abilities.

"I think it would be best if you got some sleep too. No sense in trying to do anything else. I can't port, and there's not much you can do either until you get your strength back."

Sael nodded, his head and eyes already drooping.

Chapter 15

JERIK WAS NOT IN sight when Sael awoke, but faint noises were coming from the draped section. He rose quietly and went near it.

"Jerik?"

"What?"

"What time is it?"

"Early morning kusha 2.3." Jerik came back into the room.

"Can we leave?" Sael asked.

"As far as I know."

"Then the drug's worn off?"

"Not completely, but I think I can port. Your channels feeling back in proper order?"

Sael nodded.

"Okay. Try getting a fix on the ship. I've unwarped the room, so you shouldn't have any problem."

Sael tried and found a fix easily. "It feels a lot more stable than before."

"You keep exercising your channels as you have during

the past fifteen kushas, and you'll notice more change than that. Go on, get up to the ship. I'll follow."

Within moments Sael was on the bridge, and not long afterward Jerik appeared, seated comfortably in the white command chair. The proximate glanced across to the various stations, assuring himself that everything was ready, and then over at Adia.

"Any variance in this segment of the time warp?" he asked her.

"None. We're set for the jump if we can get away."

"Mmm. Picked up any special orders from Zarth?"

She nodded. "They think you're still down below and that we're not moving out because you aren't aboard. However, he's ordered continuous surveillance on us and stationed another ship on guard. Any moves toward the warp, and they're to destroy us or, if they can't, to follow us and draw us into the energy band." She switched to private. *"I picked up some thoughts that you, yourself, gave one of their council members a deathblow."*

Jerik's face was impenetrable.

"They sent out a general alert for you two." She eyed him carefully, hoping for an explanation.

"Later," he said bluntly.

"Jerik, you've refused to tell me—"

"Consider it a false report! Get your attention back on what we're doing!"

He turned to his front-board navigator, a stable red-haired woman. "Hedra, estimate our margin of surprise and safety margin for entry into the warp."

"Our greatest margin for escape is 0.02 point," said the navigator. "We will have to pull into the warp at top entry speed with emergency slowing in order to make it in without blowing ourselves to infinity. We've got that plotted as optimum. With Lidra and Councillor Adia using their kinesis to shove the energy band out of the way, we should come through all right."

"We may need their power against the kinetics aboard

those ships. All stations, keep manual override open. Sael, get your kinesis in line with Adia's and Lidra's. We'll need everything you can supply."

Sael didn't respond. Jerik swiveled his chair and saw him in a half trance. His eyes narrowed as he joined with him mentally.

"Sael!"

Sael's eyes snapped open. *"They're going to overcome us no matter what course of action we take! If we bounce the warp, they'll overpower our kinesis and shove us into the energy band; or if we do make it in there, they will prevent us from entering the warp itself, and we won't be able to break free of the band. The only choice we have is to alter our flight plan."*

The proximate looked at him evenly. *"It won't happen that way."*

Sael stared at him.

"Don't think about it anymore. You are to help Adia and Lidra force against those time riders and move the energy band when we get to it, so put everything, and I mean absolutely everything, from your mind: premonitions, flashes, everything. Channel up with Adia. Now."

"What about the flash?"

Jerik turned back to the front of the bridge, indicating the subject was closed. *"It wasn't real."*

"But it was!"

"That's enough!"

The authoritative thought ripped through Sael, jolting his reactive emotions to life. Despite his incredible effort of control, rage overtook sane thought. That flash had been real!

A sudden thought punctured his fury. *"I told you to connect up with Adia. Do it. Now!"*

Sael said nothing, knowing he would not be able to control himself if he stayed on the bridge. Something began to give within his channels. In sudden horror of knowing what would happen if it were released, he tried to hold it back. Why didn't the proximate understand? The drug must still be affecting his mind, Sael thought.

"*Sael! Connect up!*"

He wouldn't join the mind link until Jerik realized his mistake. Resolute, he shoved his negative answer at the councilman. Immediately Sael was encompassed by an overwhelming power.

"*You are dismissed from this crew. I am turning you over to security. You will obey their orders, or you'll regret ever having acted against them.*"

As the thought ended, Sael's sense of balance slipped and twisted out from under him. Then he was in a bare room with no door and only a small floor cot. He ran toward the small, thick window set into one of the slick gray walls. Two guards stood stiffly outside, facing away from the window. He tried channeling his rage at them, but it was flung aside and twisted along a dead end by their powerful mental coercion.

"Why?" he cried. "It is you who are wrong. You! Not I! You'll burn in the energy band. I tried to warn you! Why didn't you listen?"

The silence in the room and the deathly quiet in his mind were his only answers. Turning, he rammed his kinesis at the cot, shoving it wickedly against the farthest wall, crumpling the lightweight frame, not caring what happened to them now. At war with himself, he was not aware that they had begun moving rapidly away from the planet and the two ships guarding them.

Because the crew of the *Silver Nebula* had chosen a well-planned point, when it detected loss of watchfulness on the part of its captors, its surprise tactic worked at first, but the safety margin was closing quickly. Twice they felt the jar on the ship as the kinetics aboard the other vessels worked to pull them back. Each time Councillor Adia and Lidra managed to sever the line.

They neared the time warp and, to Jerik's dismay,

would be forced to risk a full-speed entry with both the energy band and the force from the time riders to contend with. Why had Sael chosen this particular time, when his additional power was needed, to ride out his faulty premonition? Jerik groaned silently. Adia would rake him cold about the youth now, and she was probably right. He never should have insisted that the unstable come aboard.

The distortion field of the energy band loomed dangerously close on the sensor board, and Jerik suddenly knew the answer to the minute deviation in Sael's flash. Untrained and overshadowed by rising emotions, Sael couldn't detect it at the time, but Jerik had not been able to plot how the deviation would affect their outcome. Now he knew.

"Adia, let everything ride! Free-flight helmsman, navigator, manual override. Bounce the warp!" His thoughts jammed into their minds. Controls on the bridge panels were activated in unison, and the ship hit the warp and bounced over it with a jarring shock.

The time riders were unprepared for that. They had already slackened speed slightly for a smooth, even entry into the warp and noticed too late that the *Silver Nebula* had not penetrated. They attempted a course change to match it.

Councillor Adia and Lidra grasped the split moment of panic aboard the two pursuing ships and shoved their kinesis at the crews. Caught off guard by the kinetic blow and already slipping into the energy band surrounding the warp, their attempted course change ended in disaster. Within a fraction of a point they were annihilated.

Jerik ordered the ship to be brought around slowly. "Replot for entrance at our current position. Let's take it a little easier this time."

They headed toward the warp at a safer inclination and speed, their only concern being to prevent the energy

144

band from passing through the ship. Both Lidra and Adia watched for it, but Sael, in his confinement, saw it first.

Unwillingly Sael had realized that Jerik had been right. There could be things unforeseen in flashes, and looking back on it, he could see the deviation at the end. Awed by the proximate's ability to spot it while his attention was on other matters, Sael forgot his anger and was ashamed of his own stupidity and arrogance.

Simultaneously the first awareness of greater trouble hit him. The precognition wrenched him from all other thoughts, and he swung it forcibly into focus. The energy band surrounding the ship glowed with fierceness he'd not seen before, having been intensified by the destruction of the two vessels. Swollen tremendously, the brilliant blue energy would fill the ship with a field so intense it would kill them all.

Sael shut his eyes in deep concentration, found Adia's channeling, and linked up with her and Lidra. His power flowed into the expertly controlled channel, contributing to their efforts against the fierce blueness enveloping the ship. The *Silver Nebula* shuddered continuously until at last the band gave way to their combined forces and moved clear of the hull. They continued pushing it farther out until . . . suddenly it wasn't. The ship passed into the time warp, and they were riding it safely.

Exhausted, Sael sank to the floor. It occurred to him that the people of this time specialized in telekinesis to avoid contact with the band and keep it clear of their ships.

On the bridge Jerik, still keeping tight control over his crew, wondered if they would ever arrive in the time segment they wanted. But as they eased back through the warp, no mind probes from time riders tugged at them, and soon they emerged from the warp 157.336 years from their own time, a full day before the single ship from this era would warp into the past to destroy

Lym. They had to stop it! That thought filled each mind.
Somehow . . .

His navigator's voice interrupted the thought. "Councillor, there is a ship approaching the warp out at 479 degrees off our present course."

Chapter 16

SO THEIR ARRIVAL HAD not gone undetected, Jerik thought grimly. A rash move now, he told himself, and their mission would be for nothing. Lym would be devastated.

He sat back, working to catch any thoughts from those aboard the vessel. What he discovered did not ease his concern. "Balsk," he said to his helmsman, "elude them. Head out to deep space, course 0090; half speed. After 2 points set in a random course, heading in the general direction of 9089. Keep all shields up. Adia, get into a Code Three mind link with Weapons Officer Seffra. Prepare to fire at 0.04 on port. Lock that in."

Tension on the bridge seemed to crackle.

"They're tracing us," said his helmsman.

"9 over 6-mark speed increase," Jerik responded.

The *Silver Nebula* vaulted ahead, widening the gap. Suddenly the ship jerked with the telekinetic pull from those in the black vessel.

"Kinetics, sever their waves!" Jerik said.

"Unable to." Adia grimaced, concentrating on slicing the telekinetic bond slowing the *Silver Nebula*. "There are too many fighting us."

A lavender beam flashed out from the black vessel. Adia and the kinetics linked under her struggled to block the kinetically guided beam but could not completely divert it. It struck their aft shields and ruptured one.

Immediately, Adia mentally traced the beam back to its source. Seffra waited tensely, ready to fire the instant Adia gave the command. The councilwoman reached for the weaponry officer aboard the other ship. His thoughts were tightly jammed, but by probing infinitesimal lapses in the jamming, Adia knew the instant he would fire.

"*Now!*" Seffra received Adia's thought and fired.

The vessel was about to release its second volley of fire when the *Silver Nebula*'s powerful pressor beam, guided by kinesis, jarred it off course, causing the destructive beam to miss its target.

"Helm, full speed, heading 7906!" said Jerik, glancing at the scanner. Then something caught his attention and he took a second, closer, look. "Belay that. Head back on the course I originally gave you." Jerik watched the scanner for a full point. He frowned. "They're not following us."

It took the proximate a point to figure out the other ship's actions. By all rights it should have had the *Silver Nebula* running half out of the system by now. Yet it veered away from the attack and back to the warp. . . . This was *the* ship! And it was more concerned with preparations for the run into the past than with wasting time chasing the *Silver Nebula*.

Well, he had one day to figure out how to keep it from riding the warp. The privacy of his quarters seemed as good a place as any to work on it since he wouldn't be needed on the bridge immediately. He rose from the white command chair. "Balsk, run your course for another 3 kushas. Then plot a linear course to 4003 and from there back to the warp at a 5-degree inclination. When you near the warp, keep well out of their sensor range. Adia"—he turned to the councilwoman—"well done on reading that weaponry officer. I'll never understand how you can detect that close, especially under as stiff a mind guard as they had set up."

"Practice," she said blandly.

"For that," he retorted, "you keep watch on the bridge. I have other matters to attend to." With that the proximate ported off the bridge.

Twenty-seven points later Jerik was lying on his bed in the quiet of his cabin. He had eaten, showered, changed clothes, and also managed to wrap up some routine problems. He suddenly remembered that Sael was still confined in the security chamber, and an annoyed look crossed his face as he thought of the youth. Jerik ordered the guards to release him.

"Come to my quarters, Sael."

Two points later he got a telepathic query from the young man.

"Come in."

The door opened, and Sael walked in hesitantly. "Yes, Councillor?"

"Well, come in all the way, so I can talk with you."

The door slid shut.

Exhausted, the proximate lay back on his bed with one arm resting across his shut eyes. His left leg was bent up slightly, and he didn't move as Sael approached. Remnants of the drug he'd been given were still affecting him. Maybe that future time did not exist right now, but what he had carried back into the present in his body remained.

"Sit down."

Sael sat in the nearest chair he could find. "Sir . . . I'm sorry I—"

"Hold your silence."

Sael closed his mouth, hardly daring even to look at the councilman. They both were quiet for a long time.

After three points Sael began to wonder if Jerik had fallen asleep. He had neither moved nor spoken.

When at last he did speak, his voice was soft, but its tone severe. "I suppose I should thank you for helping Kinetic Technician Lidra and Councillor Adia push the energy band away from the ship. Consider yourself thanked."

"Sir, I—"

"I said, consider yourself thanked!" Jerik snapped. He lay in exactly the same position.

Sael looked down. "Yes, Councillor."

There was another long pause. Jerik spoke out again. "You gave the security guards a rough time, I understand."

"I did."

"And you're not ashamed of it?"

"I am, Councillor."

Again there was a pause. Then: "You were told twice your premonition was false and still disbelieved me. Why?"

"I don't know," he whispered.

"You were so stuck on having your way that you couldn't possibly conceive that maybe for once you were wrong. Am I right?" He received no answer and sat up slightly, fixing his eyes forcefully on Sael. "I said, am I right?"

Sael could only nod, feeling self-conscious before the proximate.

Jerik lay back with his arm resting over his eyes again. "Do you really mean that or are you just agreeing with me to get me off your mind?"

"I mean that, Councillor. I saw I was wrong in the security block."

"I gave you an order on the bridge. Why did you disobey it?"

"I don't know. I guess I couldn't understand why you disregarded my flash, and then my instability hit me."

150

"It was your blasted arrogance that hit you! I saw you were wrong, and we had a job to perform. That's why I had you confined when you blew up at me. I couldn't let your silly tantrum interfere with the execution of our actions!"

"I understand."

Jerik glared at him again. "Do you? Do you really understand what your self-centered assertions nearly caused? Do you know what would have happened if I hadn't passed a check over your premonition? Well? And when you decided you'd had enough of me . . ."

"Sir, I couldn't help it! I tried to stop, but I couldn't!"

"Then you had better learn," Jerik snapped. "And you had better learn now. Because you've cut your chances of ever being out in space again to nil. When you are in the middle of an emergency, there is no time for personal feelings. You don't play with arrogance and self-assertions and likes or dislikes or anything else. You have a job and you perform it, or you don't make it at all. When you are in the middle of any emergency situation, you *don't* let your thoughts wander off on every half-moon flippancy that pops into your head! You execute! You perform! Flawlessly. Immediately. There's no room for anything else! You simply do whatever it takes. Have you got that?"

"Yes, sir," Sael mumbled.

Jerik grunted and lay back. "Now, if you think that just possibly you can be inclined to exercise a little more self-restraint, I might decide to release you from security. I'm not saying all premonitions you get must be suppressed or anything like that. But when you're given a direct order, at least have the decency and intelligence to carry it out instead of acting like a half-wit!"

The insult brought Sael's head up, but he said nothing beyond "I will."

"Leave me then," Jerik said wearily. "And consider yourself released from security. But on strict probation."

Sael rose and headed toward the door. As he reached it, he turned back to the proximate, searching for words, but all that came out was: "Yes, sir." Then he left the room.

Depressed, Sael wandered down the corridor, making his way to the ship's diner. He ordered something to eat, but when the food came he had no appetite. Although he had not eaten since the councillor had given him the protein complex the night before, he left the order in a reconverter bin.

Sael went back to his small quarters and sank down on the bed. When one pledged support, he gave it. His promise to the proximate had been broken with his actions on the bridge. Jerik had, of course, dealt with him in the only right way, but what could he, Sael, do to reestablish the confidence and trust of the councilman?

For the next kusha Sael tried reading, anything to take his mind off the problem. Absentmindedly he punched something into the small console and waited for the readouts to appear on the screen. He never saw them, though. He continued to fret at the cause of his own unruly behavior.

When he could no longer sit there, pretending to read, he rose and went to the bridge. It was quiet. The shift had changed, although Councillor Adia was still working at her board. Sael paused a moment, decided, then approached her.

She sensed him coming and turned in her chair slightly, giving him a look that made it plain she thought he had no business on the bridge in light of his recent actions.

"May I talk with you, Councillor?"

She considered for a while, then gave him a curt nod.

"I want to apologize for refusing to help you earlier."

"Your apology is to be directed to Councillor Jerik, not me."

"I already tried to. I never should have let myself get that far out of control. Please understand I mean it when

I say I realize I was wrong, and why." His pale-green eyes earnestly met hers.

She continued to watch him as he looked away. "So you do," she said bluntly, and was silent for a time, then added, "You've never encountered the strict discipline of a starship in action and the guiding of your powers at the same time. Just watch yourself." Adia turned back to her console.

Sael grew quiet for a point, watching her, thinking about her words. "What's our course heading now?"

"0302; mark 8 speed. We'll be in range of the time warp in approximately 1.3 kushas."

He watched her console flicker and flash its various readouts. "From here to our time the warp is unstable. Why?"

Annoyance crossed her face. Nevertheless, she answered him while continuing to work with her board. "It has to do with the flux of hyperspace. Its distortion field is the only one we've ever run across. That's what we think caused the time warp in the first place, though we have not discovered why; it was one of the side purposes of this mission. But we do know from our last penetration that violent fluctuation and instability in the warp can be generated by turbulence created within it or the energy band."

Sael was lost in thought as he continued to watch her computations flash across the boards, remembering the agitation of the band. "Councillor, what would happen if something were to explode inside the warp itself?"

"Be more specific."

"Well, I was thinking about those two ships we pulled into the energy band. It became dangerously swollen and almost sealed us off from our entry into the warp. I was wondering what would happen if a ship were to explode in the warp."

She looked at him sharply, and he added hastily, "Not *us*, of course. I mean one of their ships." He jerked his head in the direction of the viewscreen.

Adia suddenly caught his train of thought and surprised herself by agreeing with it. "In the unstable segment of the warp it should seal it off completely."

"Which would mean time travel along the warp wouldn't exist." Eagerness raced through Sael. "It might even obliterate the warp. That ship wouldn't be able to come back into the past and destroy Lym!"

For a moment Adia's dark eyes shone, and then they grew serious. "But how do we work it so we don't get trapped in the warp ourselves? We'd have to pull that ship after us, and we'd be traveling the warp when the explosion disrupted it."

Sael sobered up. "I hadn't thought of that."

"It's still not a bad idea. I'd rather be a pile of antimatter than have Galapix destroyed."

He wasn't sure he liked that part of the idea at all. But if there was no other way . . .

"Sael, let's see what we can come up with anyway," said Adia, temporarily forgetting past antagonism. "When Councillor Jerik gets back up here, he can give us his views, but I want to have something ready for him." She extended a hand toward one of the consoles next to hers. "Get with it."

They had been working steadily with his theory and were still computing the finer details when the bridge door opened and Jerik, looking haggard, walked through. He was astonished to find Sael in deep conference with Adia.

He strode over, determined not to show his surprise. "What's so terribly fascinating between you two that you can't let me in on it?"

Sael turned to face the proximate, excited. "We think we've found a way to break the warp."

"What in the fringe of the universe are you talking about?"

Adia glanced up. "He's right. Only it isn't 'we,' it's him. Look at this." She showed Jerik the readouts they had compiled, explaining as she went, but the proximate didn't need explanation after the first few figures.

Adia was not satisfied, though. "If we fire at them in the warp, we'll be trapped in there permanently with the black vessel."

A slight smile crossed Jerik's features. "Simple," he said. "We rig up a couple of int bombs with delayed reaction plugs, fuse them into their quando-drive mechanism and siblar reactor in the engineering control center, and get into the warp with enough of a margin to put us a few months ahead of them. It means a rough ride and bad braking at the end, but we'll come out all right as long as we don't let anything slip. Then, while they're still in the warp and we're well out of it, they'll explode. 'Course, it should seal, if not collapse, the entire thing. It's perfectly simple," he said, walking to the ultra-cush command chair. But he wondered just how perfectly simple it would be.

Chapter 17

JERIK DID NOT AGAIN mention Sael's presence on
the bridge, nor did he pay the young man any attention
during the remainder of the flight back to the warp. In
his mind he saw the black ship guarding the time warp
and making extensive preparations toward riding it
into the past to destroy Lym. He saw that telepathy and
other key abilities of the people of this era, aside from
telekinesis, were on a downward trend. That was one
factor in his favor. However, when provoked, they were
ruthless in attack. Not that Jerik wouldn't be also, but
he didn't want to expend time and energy in battle.

Death of that ship's crew by a massive attack of
thought-crushing telepathy was out of the question. The
proximate did not have enough penetration telepathists
on board to launch such an assault, and more important,
killing the crew would not seal the warp so no other time
rider could penetrate it. No, he had to lure that ship
into the warp behind the *Silver Nebula*, using it as a
weapon to seal, if not collapse, the time warp.

The only matter that worried him was the kinetic pull

of those aboard the black vessel if they did not get into the warp soon enough. It had been stronger than even he had anticipated. The vessel would pursue, but both ships had to enter the warp before the kinetics took hold of the *Silver Nebula*.

Jerik carefully plotted his action. He knew how he would go about it. And the outcome? He checked his channels and found them dark. Both sides were so perfectly balanced that either could win, and his channels would not govern the decision. Very rarely did he find himself riding blind as to what would happen. He didn't relish it. He could not even be certain the explosion would destroy the entire warp. There were not enough data for that, although there was solid indication that it would collapse their end.

"Sael." He motioned to the young man.

As Sael came over, Jerik looked at the central viewscreen, knowing that out there death waited for one future or the other. Would it be his or theirs? As if in response, the stars shone harshly against the stark black background. "Sael," he said slowly, his gaze still fixed on the screen, "I have a job for you."

"Sir?" he asked.

"A way for you to make up for your actions. Besides, you're the only one who can do it." Jerik finally looked at him. "We are going to head into the warp, provoking that ship into following us. Before we do, you are going to port to it on my channel, not on yours, and place and arm two int bombs: one in their quando-drive and the other to their siblar reactor. We don't have to worry about their detecting you porting in, not if we do this correctly, but it's going to be close for you at the end. By the time you've activated those ints we'll be getting fully into the warp. If we're in the warp while you are still on that ship, you won't be able to port back because the *Silver Nebula* will have moved out of the time continuum. Think you are willing to risk that?" he asked in a voice that implied he already knew the answer.

There was no question in Sael's mind. "With full responsibility, sir," he replied.

"Okay. When you get there, you'll have to rely on yourself as much as possible. I don't want to risk intership telepathy at this stage unless I have to. Now let me brief you on where to set the bombs. Their engineering room is different from ours. Their quando-drive is basically the same. but their reactor is set up with very poor safety guards, and it's arranged in a more complex pattern."

Jerik went on to explain to Sael what he had mentally analyzed earlier and gave him explicit instructions through transfer telepathy. Sael nodded and was on the verge of porting to the weapons area when Jerik stopped him.

"Don't. You'll be porting back from that ship on your own. Let your power relax. You'll need it later."

Tension already mounting, Sael left the bridge on foot.

Jerik watched him go, feeling vaguely guilty for not telling him exactly how close the margin would be. Setting the bombs was one thing; activating them was another. The power surge would be monitored on the bridge of the vessel, and since they wouldn't know the cause, they would investigate. Sael would barely have enough time to activate the ints and port back to the ship. Again, Jerik went over in his mind exactly what would happen. Just before activation, the *Silver Nebula* would lure the black ship to the warp. And Sael would have to port across the changing distance, something he had never done. The proximate turned his attention back to the screen. That would happen in its own good time. He had other things to worry about right now.

Sael's nervousness increased as he approached the guarded weapons area. The walk had not been that long, but it was enough to give him time to realize himself exactly how little time he would have.

At the weapons area the security guard let him pass. As the doors closed behind him, he glanced across the room. At the far end on a metal table sat two small octagonal boxes with three connectors each. He went over to them and picked them up. Small enough to fit in his closed hand, he thought, yet one alone had the power to rip half the atmosphere off a world. They felt light in his hand. Their destructive potential weighed heavily on his mind.

His wait for Jerik's order was not long. Within ten points he felt the proximate's powerful mind join his.

"We expect trouble from that ship. When you set those int bombs, wait for my signal to activate them."

Sael's mouth went dry. His thoughts were as unresponsive as his voice.

"Get into my channel. Now."

In full contact with Jerik's mind, he saw the channel open wide before him. It still harbored a few wisps of the drug the councillor had been exposed to, and they bothered Sael and made him lose his concentration.

"Don't fight it! Just get in the channel and push past it."

The channel was locked shut as he entered. He was fully in and then through. . . .

Sael found himself in a dark corner in the master engineering section of the black vessel. An eerie pale-lavender light was cast throughout the room, accentuating deep shadows and seeming to enlarge and distort the rows of equipment. A steady, pulsating sibilation wheezed from somewhere before him. He remembered Jerik telling him that this section was totally automated and wondered why they didn't post even one guard. With perfect clarity, he recalled the pattern of the room and the units he had to reach and began making his way slowly along the narrow corridor between two large slick-surfaced units.

As he emerged from between them, he saw a large globular object suspended in a clear cubicle and knew that was the heart of the siblar reactor: the power center of the engine's quando-drive. The brilliant pale-lavender light emitting from it hurt his eyes as he moved past it. First to the quando-drive, then the reactor, and then back to the quando-drive to activate the primary int on Jerik's word and then port back. It was very simple, he told himself repeatedly. Nonetheless, a horrible knot clenched his stomach, and he felt sick.

He came to the outer panel of the quando-drive mechanism. Placing the int bombs down, he tentatively reached into one of the eight hand chambers and eased the inner pullcase out. It made no sound. Everything was quiet save for the rhythmical sss-sss-ssssss from the reactor. The counter connector leads he wanted were aligned toward the rear of the inside of the case. He took the primary int and, working as quickly as stealth and nervousness would allow, fixed the three connectors of the bomb to the main components in the case. The tiny bomb itself remained suspended in its own delicately balanced stasis field.

Now to the reactor. Sael reached the pale-lavender, glowing, encased sphere, carefully shielding his eyes from its naked fury. It had a highly charged invisible force shield surrounding it, energized by its own power. Sael was not sure exactly how far from the cubicle the field extended. He could only sense and hope his guess was accurate.

The reactor stood on a triangular base. The base, he knew, had no shield around it, but the reactor's force shield extended dangerously close to it. The fourth level of the seven-level base held the connecting leads he needed. He crept around the force shield and knelt on the floor because it was the only way he could reach it. Then, suddenly, the vessel shook, knocking him off balance. He lurched toward the reactor and tried desperately to avoid hitting its shield, but as he regained his footing, his right arm touched it slightly. Bluish-green sparks flashed on contact. Sael nearly cried out in pain as he pulled away, clamped his mouth shut, and sank weakly to the floor, looking numbly at his arm. One side of it, along with the back of his hand, was blackened. For a long time he sat huddled against the base of one of the other drive units, thinking wildly that someone had detected him as he mentally cried out in anguish. The searing pain was something he could not move telekinetically.

Sael's attention was still on his burned arm and hand when he realized he had not placed the int bomb. Crawling back to the reactor base, his right arm dragging uselessly at his side, he remembered how simple he had thought this would be. But now he had only one useful hand and was having trouble concentrating. Pain. Everything was mind-racking pain. He was in a dizzying lavender world of eerie distortions and agony. He scarcely felt the bomb in his good hand. As if in a dream, Sael watched himself set it down on the floor and then slowly, one by one, release the connectors of the leads in the reactor base, hold the bomb in place until its stasis field took over, and refasten the connectors.

With the last one fixed in place, Sael sank weakly to the floor face down. The warm, hard surface offered no relief to the pain flooding his mind. The lavender turned to furious yellow when he shut his eyes. Dimly he wondered why the ship had shaken. Weariness seeped through his body. The pain, like a million white hot needles tormenting his flesh, suddenly shrank to a distant throbbing echo as he lost consciousness.

Something reverberated in the black halls of his mind, and then with more strength it shook the darkness off.

"Sael!" The call was urgent, demanding. *"Get up! You've got to get to the quando and activate that int! Now! Sael!"*

The tone pried him awake. Infuriating, blinding pain returned full force. Clenching his teeth against it, he rose unsteadily and made his way step by step to the quando-drive unit. It loomed before him in hazy distortion. He fumbled for the int bomb in the exposed hand case and set the activator core on the preset time release. The only thing left to do was to port back now. . . .

Sael shook his head, and a tired smile crossed his face. Port back, he thought. That was funny. He could hardly stand, and he was supposed to port back. He even made a futile attempt to show himself how ridiculous it was. He let his body sink down alongside the quando chamber. Faintly in the back of his mind he thought he heard Jerik calling him. He closed his thoughts to it with the pain.

"I can't," he whispered to himself in growing delirium. "I can't. I am sorry, Jerik. I'm sorry about disbelieving you and getting angry with you and everything." Sael looked at his seared hand and arm through blurred eyes. "But you'll have your past. You've made it. You've . . ." Darkness washed over him. At the same moment he felt something tugging at him. Someone from the vessel had found him. They must never discover the int bombs. But it was useless. He felt dizzy. Terribly nauseated. As though the universe were exploding from under him. His head hit something solid. Blackness swept down on him, and he knew no more.

Chapter 18

THE BRIDGE OF THE *Silver Nebula* was a flurry of orders and actions as the crew fought to lure the black vessel into the warp behind them. Intent on penetrating the warp, Jerik was also aware that Sael was still aboard the other ship, wallowing on the edge of unconsciousness.

"*Adia!*" he flashed, sensing her hands moving to the controls of her board to bring the ship into the warp. "*NO! Wait!*"

She was astounded by his abrupt contrary order, and sheer amazement stayed her hands. That instant was all Jerik needed to lock onto Sael across the distance and brace himself. He concentrated with lightning fury. His power lashed across the gulf of space to the black ship and brought Sael back with it, depositing him roughly on the bridge floor. The ship's main surgeon, Raien, had been forewarned, and he took Sael over from there and transported him down to sick bay.

Jerik now was oblivious to that. "*Adia, get with it! Full-speed entry! Lidra, channel your kinesis at the energy band. Now!*"

The *Silver Nebula* ran straight for the time warp. The black vessel, unaware of its destructive cargo, raced in pursuit. Jerik knew his only option was to risk a top-speed entry into the warp. As long as Lidra could keep the pressure of the energy band off the hull with her kinesis, they might make it through. He wished Sael could have merged his power with hers.

They rammed against the band with a force that shook the ship. Somehow, enough pressure was relieved from the hull to allow the ship to pass into the warp itself. They were alone, away from the vessel, and at their speed 157.336 years required immediate braking.

"Adia, freeze all controls!"

Her telekinesis strained to slow the ship. Lidra, no longer fighting the energy band, trained her attention on the heart of the ship and fabric of the hull to prevent the strain from ripping it apart. In less than two points the *Silver Nebula* jolted, trying to break loose from the warp. Every panel on the bridge was threatened with overload. Two of them did, and a third was on the verge of it when, with a final shock, the ship virtually catapulted out of the warp and into normal space.

The *Silver Nebula* drifted as though dead in space. The bridge was in chaos. The rest of the ship was not much better off. Most of the bridge crew had been thrown. Miraculously, the field locks on three had held. Jerik, although stunned, was still at his post when a flash suddenly ripped through his channel with gripping reality.

Four years from the present time, the black vessel, still inside the warp, detonated. The energy band crumpled into the time warp, shattered into visible cracks, fractured the time continuum, and shot the warp into jagged blue fragments throughout the spatial sector.

The shocking intensity of the premonition and its validity stupefied Jerik.

Adia had not been thrown and, although dazed, was

the first to take charge. A glance at the boards told her the main life-support system was in shaky but temporarily acceptable condition throughout most of the ship. She released her lock and went first to Jerik, put her hands on his face, and tried to reach him mentally.

Struggling back to his senses, he felt the last effects of the drug in his mind and her hands on him. Fight! That was his first thought. Fight! His head felt strange, but that didn't matter. Fight! He grabbed her arms roughly.

"Hey! I was only trying to help!"

He peered at her. Recognition came. "Adia?"

"Well, who'd you think it was?"

He shook his head to clear it as he sat up. "Nobody," he mumbled, not loud enough for her to hear.

"Well?"

"No one," he said crossly. He didn't want to be reminded of Azella again. "You startled me, that's all."

"Some startle," she muttered under her breath as she went to one of the other fallen crew members. Jerik stood up and went to help a crewman who was attempting to sit up. "You okay?" he asked, extending a steadying hand.

The crewman nodded.

Jerik glanced about the room. The bridge looked like the aftermath of a battle. "Lidra? Gaelak? Hedra?"

They were shaken but uninjured.

"Adia, what's our life support look like?" he asked, walking carefully over some debris to her empty station. He rubbed his left shoulder, which had been hurt in the initial shock when the ship broke through the warp.

"Sixty-two percent functional with an intermittent fluctuation down to twenty percent," she called to him from across the bridge, where she was busy at another board.

He muttered unintelligibly under his breath, punched several figures into the console, and grunted at the response. "I want a full damage report as soon as possible and all the power we can spare routed down to sick bay. Don't contact the Council until we know where we stand . . . and when," he added. He went to another station and began a check with it.

Twenty-three points later he ported off the bridge. By then the bridge crew members were back at their posts, receiving the inflow of damage reports and coordinating repair teams.

Jerik had ported down to sick bay and headed into the main surgical lab. Raien and his relatively small staff had enough casualties on their hands, though most conditions were not serious. The surgeon, finishing with one patient, noticed Jerik as he entered the area and pointed a warning finger at the councilman.

"You, if you're on two feet, you don't belong here. Get out."

Jerik knew that when Raien was working, he did not like to be approached by anyone who was not flat on his back. Nevertheless, Jerik approached him.

"Sael. I want to know how he is."

"I told you. Get out! Unless you want to stick your consciousness into eighteen minds and straighten them out. Not to mention getting your hands in their blood and guts." The surgeon had moved beside another patient and was standing over him with deep intent, mentally searching for the origin of pain.

Jerik waited. Several of Raien's assistants came and went into other parts of the lab area, where, Jerik knew, others waited for treatment, either by the staff or Raien himself.

After about three points Raien, still intent over his patient, stirred and relaxed. He walked away from the platform and out of the corner of his eye caught Jerik standing by the open doorway. "Look, I told you . . ."

"What about Sael?" Jerik's deep gray eyes met the surgeon's.

The surgeon returned the look impatiently. "He's under deradiation and neural surgery. He'll have to have complete skin restoration on his right hand and arm when we get back to Galapix."

The answer did not satisfy the proximate. "Have you been able to reach him mentally?"

The surgeon shook his head as if he didn't want to talk about it and started toward another patient.

The proximate's look held him.

Unwillingly Raien continued. "I can't get through to to him. I tried before he went into surgery. He's so deeply entwined in his channels I can't even find him."

Jerik eyed Raien quietly. "How much longer is he going to be under deradiation?"

"No. I know what you want. I can't allow it this time. Jerik, he's too deep!"

"I've been in his mind before. I know where he goes when he blacks out."

"It isn't just a matter of simple unconsciousness! He's trapped down in all that muck somewhere."

"I can get to him."

"You're no surgeon!"

"When he gets out of deradiation," said Jerik, intensity edging in his voice, "you let me know."

Raien had already left the room.

Jerik ported back to the bridge and found it in somewhat better shape than when he had left. At least his crew looked more alert. He moved over to Adia, who was working with her console.

"Casualties in sick bay?" she asked without turning to look at him.

"Eighteen. I won't try to estimate how many are lying about the ship dead."

"Twenty-two," she said flatly.

His eyes widened.

She felt his look. Still busy with her board, she continued. "We ruptured the outer hull along section two, deck nine. The inner locks sealed, but we lost seventeen there. The other five were in engineering when a line broke. I'm surprised we didn't lose more."

He nodded. "What do we look like for repairs?"

"Either we sit here for the next two months, trying to unjam our fused quando, or we call for a tow ship." She cast aside the delicate instrument she was futilely attempting to use on her open board. "I don't know why we still have life support at all. We shouldn't. There's an intermittent catch in the antigrav field, and we're holding out on trickle power from the main reactor. When that goes, so do we." She looked down at the open mass of circuitry before her. "Eighty-three percent of the total functioning capacity of this ship is out. We burned, fused, overloaded, and all but ripped her in two."

Jerik tried to ignore the bitterness in her voice. "When are we?"

"Six days from when we first entered the warp, fourteen days from our departure from Galapix."

"What's the estimated time to get this hulk moving again?"

Her mouth twitched. "The quando-drive is out. I told you that."

"I mean sublight speed."

"Sublight? It would take us a good three weeks. You tore this ship apart coming through that warp." Her eyes came up and met his. "Jerik, if you hadn't insisted on waiting until the last possible instant, we wouldn't be in this mess. We didn't have to hit the warp at full speed!"

"I couldn't leave him behind," he muttered.

Willing to agree for once without further argument, Adia looked down. "I've already contacted the Council," she said softly.

"I said not to—"

"—until we knew where we stood," she finished for him. "We know that now. Anyway, they knew we had emerged from the warp. I just gave them a damage report. Hedrick wanted more info, and he wanted to speak with you. I told him you were busy. I didn't give him anything else."

Jerik eyed her askance. "You? Clamming up on Hedrick? Maybe you got jolted by the throw from the time warp."

"Maybe for once I think you're right," she said quietly.

"About what?" He was genuinely nonplussed at her sincerity.

"About Sael."

He grew silent at that and gave her a wondering look before telling her to micro-beam all the mission reports to the Interworld Council on Galapix. Then he moved on to the other stations on the bridge.

Twenty points later he received a mental call from Raien. He teleported immediately to sick bay, found the surgeon heading into one of the small private rooms off the main surgical lab, and followed him in. Raien led him to the platform where Sael lay. Very gently Jerik opened his mind to the young man. Sael did not respond. Worry growing, Jerik tried it again. It hadn't been like this previously when Sael had been unconscious; then Sael had refused to respond. Now he simply wasn't responding . . . or couldn't.

Sael was totally confused. He was spinning in terror, fleeing from something unidentified, and every time he tried to orient himself confusion swirled over him and he'd hide again in the blackness. But the blackness was no longer comforting. It, too, was turbulent. He was more alone and afraid than he could remember ever being. Vaguely Sael realized that he had a choice between remaining in limbo, drifting toward death, or confronting the unknown terror of massive confusion and, holding fast to his sanity, pushing through it to life.

Yet what kind of life awaited him? One to be plagued with irreparable disorientation so thorough it would leave him unable to give or receive communication? One that

169

would leave him mentally and physically disabled despite what surgery could accomplish? And in what time did he exist? All sense of time had been lost. Had it been moments or hours since he'd set the bombs? If he was in the future, he wanted no part of that. Death was the only way out, and would occur soon if he'd set the bombs right. Had he? He couldn't remember.

Confusion swirled, and Sael tried to take refuge—anywhere. But he knew there was no refuge in the blackness, or in tears, or in this time, whenever it was. Worse, he was alone. There was no one out there. Whatever decision he had to make was his alone to make. What purpose, then, was left in life?

Jerik anxiously probed again but found nothing. "Raien, work with me. We've got to reach him."

"I'm not guaranteeing anything," said the surgeon. Nonetheless he mentally merged with Jerik. Together they probed. It was like entering a void at first, empty, motionless. Jerik and Raien searched desperately for any sign of Sael but found nothing.

"*He's gone,*" Jerik telepathed bleakly. "*It must have happened when I pulled him aboard. We were on the verge of slipping into the time warp. I pulled him as hard as I could in the time I had left.*"

"*It was too much for him,*" Raien responded.

"*But he's got to be around!*" Jerik plunged deeper into the blackness and found himself rapidly losing awareness. He fought to control and clear his thoughts. "*I'm getting so confused. . . .*" A wave of nausea swept over him. "*Raien, help me.*"

"*Jerik, that's not your confusion! It's Sael's. He's in there somewhere.*"

"*Raien, can you straighten this out?*"

"*I'd be working blind. I could kill him.*"

"*Work blind then. I'll guide you. I know his mental patterns.*"

"*I couldn't risk it.*"

"He'll die anyway if he stays like this."

Raien knew the councilman was right. *"Ride my perception. You'll have to tell me what channels I'm hitting. Brace yourself. You'll feel everything I do."*

Jerik was ready for the first sharp mental jolt. He felt dispersed by the ubiquitous confusion and was grateful for the steadying influence of the surgeon.

"I'm shoving against something. What is it?"

"That . . ." it was difficult not to succumb to the confusion. *"That is his kinesis . . . I think."*

"You've got to be absolutely certain!"

Was he positive? He hadn't really been in the young man's mind often enough to know for sure, but wait— There had been one time when he had been in perfect contact. He recalled the time and Sael's mind patterns. His channels. Exactly where they were.

"No!" Jerik said, suddenly certain. *"That's his premonition channel."*

"Okay." Raien gave the channel a kinetic push. It flexed, then straightened and came clear. Jerik had been right. The surgeon found another. *"How about this one?"*

"That's his porting. Careful, it overlaps his fix line."

Raien carefully unsnarled the two and moved on. One by one they located and identified Sael's channels, and slowly the confusion yielded to order.

Suddenly Jerik signaled. *"Raien, back out! I think I've found him. Let me deal with him alone."*

Jerik probed with precision. Something had stirred in all that murk.

"Sael? Where are you? It's Jerik. Sael, follow my thoughts. Reach out."

Something was out there. Fearfully Sael recoiled from it and held still, hoping it would go away.

"Sael! Please!" Jerik's probing brought him closer to Sael. He sensed the core of fear. Cautiously and gently he moved nearer. *"Sael? I won't hurt you. Come on, reach toward me."*

It was close now. But not frightening. It was even soothing, comforting. Safer, almost, than the rough blackness where he hid.

"Reach, Sael."

It might be safe to reach a little.

Jerik felt the reach and extended himself toward it slowly. *"Come on, give it some more."*

Obediently Sael reached out further. And Jerik extended himself slowly until they touched. The sudden contact frightened Sael, and he recoiled again. Jerik patiently started coaxing him to reach again until finally contact was maintained, and then he flowed calmness and strength to Sael until the young man let go of his terror in spasms of grief. Jerik gave him all the time he needed, accepting the deluge until it was exhausted.

Then tentatively he probed again.

Sael recognized him and surged closer, then stopped, bewildered by the confusion.

"It's okay. I've got you. Just follow me to the surface." Jerik led him back to consciousness. At the threshold of full awareness Sael grew alarmed again. His hearing was muffled, and when he opened his eyes, the nausea and disorientation returned. Up was off sideways, and down was terribly out of whack.

Sael felt Raien begin to probe in and drew back, but the surgeon held onto him, coaxing him to help continue the tedious process of completely unsnarling his channels and communication lines.

When the job was finished, Sael tiredly opened his eyes. The first person he saw was the proximate, and for a long time they simply looked at each other.

Finally Jerik broke the silence. "You made it okay."

Chapter 19

SAEL LOOKED AWAY. "You should have left me behind on that ship."

"You've pulled yourself through a lot in the past few days. I don't think you mean that."

"I meant what I said! Why didn't you just leave me alone?" He turned his head, then wished he hadn't. Nausea returned in painful force, and everything was hazy and completely off. "Just leave me alone."

"Sael . . ."

"I told you to leave! I want to die. Did you hear me? I said I want to die!" His voice had risen.

"I don't believe that."

"I don't care *what* you believe!" The world, dim and muted, spun and closed in on him. He shut his eyes.

"Sael, you are going to be all right. It's just going to take time. You've been through— You've gone from totally undisciplined powers and complete instability to accomplishing things in a few brief days no one else could have undertaken. You should have learned by now you

can't keep running from things! Remember what Palox told you? Deal with your life."

Sael couldn't shut the mental communication out.

"Remember the futures we saw?" Jerik said fiercely.

"Get out of my mind!" Sael cried.

"Remember Zarth's time? The distorted, dead world our descendants left for Palox and his people? Palox didn't deserve to live in that kind of a future."

It was impossible to avoid seeing the pictures Jerik pushed at him. It hurt to remember that time in the war-torn defeated future. The proximate had purposely sent him to the black vessel, knowing death was inevitable, and then yanked him back to prolong the agony and disrupt his stability for life. He wanted the death that had been refused him. . . .

The raw tone of Jerik's mental call wrenched Sael from the unconsciousness toward which he had been slipping. *"Remember Palox. Remember his thoughts. They were clean. And they didn't get that way because he ran from things! Remember that, Sael! You've got a chance. Confront your life and emotions, and create a new future for yourself. Death may seem the easy way out, but nothing changes unless you do something about it here and now. Make that change! We have given Galapix a new chance, a new era. Be a part of it!"*

Sael didn't respond.

Jerik turned from him, angry with himself for not making better contact and angry with Sael for succumbing. Scowling, he left sick bay.

The proximate pushed the thoughts from his mind and walked up to the bridge, telling himself he had more important things to worry about right now. When he arrived, Adia had an expectant look on her face. Jerik knew what she was going to say before she opened her mouth, and the scowl on his countenance remained.

"Hedrick wants to talk with you privately," she said.

"I know." The proximate stood for a time, his gray eyes unfocused, his expression blank. Then he frowned.

When the communication ended, he was still frowning. He went back to Adia's open board and scrutinized it. "Get any of this back in order?"

"If you call trying to knock fused lines back into their cables with a tyke-pin getting this back together, no."

"When's the tow ship scheduled to arrive?"

"Another twenty-three points. Life support is still fluctuating, but it's seventy-two percent operational now." Her thoughts melded with his. *"Jerik?"*

"Did you send the full reports to the Council?"

"Yes."

Jerik frowned again. *"Well, something's up. Hedrick's got a meeting scheduled as soon as we arrive."*

Even before the ship reached a standard docking orbit, First Councillor Hedrick's aide, Kol Lenn, ordered the two council members planetside for an immediate meeting. In the telepathic directive the aide insisted that Jerik use the electronic transport, rather than teleport.

"As per the first councillor's command," Jerik muttered. "Hedrick knows I get ill when I use that . . . that thing."

"Those were his orders."

"I know. They wouldn't be *yours*." Jerik was silent. What bothered him more than the thought of being disoriented by the transport was why the first councillor insisted on it. There was no need for that. He shook his head as they entered the transport chamber.

"Jerik . . ." Adia's look, a silent entreaty to him to forgive her past actions, held him for an instant.

He broke her gaze and waved impatiently to the technician monitoring the mechanism. "Let's get this over with. Go ahead."

His world shattered in that horrible, sickening sensation of transport. He tried to hold himself rigid against it, but in the few moments it took he became completely disoriented, as he always did when using the transporter.

Amid sickening distortions Jerik crumpled to the floor on a transport pad in the Council building. Someone grabbed him and was pulling him down, forcing him to stay on the floor. No, no. That was all wrong! Jerik made an effort to reorient himself, and things started straightening out. A green-clad security man was pulling him to his feet. Jerik's astonishment overcame his nausea for the moment. Adia must have been transported elsewhere. He, however, was in a detainment cell!

Instinctively, he pulled sharply away from the guard, though he should have known better. The guard's specially disciplined kinesis instantly held him immobile.

"What is the meaning of this? Release me immediately!"

"The Council is ready for you now, Proximate," came a new voice. "Guard, keep him under kinetic control."

Jerik would have turned if he could. Suddenly, through the transport disorientation, he recognized the voice of Hedrick's top aide. "Kol Lenn!"

"That's right, Jerik. You are under arrest." The short middle-aged man came around to Jerik's view.

Arrest! The proximate was taut, like a wire pulled too tight, visibly fighting the unwarranted kinetic hold on him. He couldn't port against the guard's power.

"For what? You have no authority—"

Kol Lenn held up one hand. "On the contrary. I have Hedrick's authority. You not only violated the first councillor's direct order by taking Sael with you, but according to Adia's report, you, as well as that unstable, had an emotional outburst, which could have ruined the mission."

"The mission has been successfully accomplished. I received no word from Hedrick about an arrest. Release me!"

"Hedrick did not make the arrest. I did. By law I am therefore the one to inform you."

"Your excuse is too thin!" flared the proximate. "Hedrick himself said there was no reason for arrest!"

"That was before Adia's report came through. You, sir"—he slurred the words—"are due for a court action.

176

Guard!" Kol Lenn snapped. The guard touched a unit on his belt, and the three transported off the pad in the detainment cell to the meeting room of the Interworld Council, where a full session had just begun.

Jerik would have fallen again if the guard had not been holding him kinetically. Now he understood why he'd been requested to transport. In the time it took to regain orientation, the guard could easily have him under control. Sheer determination overrode most of the disorientation. Jerik addressed Hedrick before anyone had a chance to speak.

"What is going on?" he demanded. "Don't you think I should have been given some clue I was being arrested? You know me well enough to know I'd face the charges without . . . this!" He tried to move his arms and could not. "Release me!"

Hedrick was about to speak when Kol Lenn intervened. "I would advise against it, sir. Your proximate's emotions are as violent as they were when he almost killed Councilwoman Adia the night before their time flight."

The room was deathly still, anticipating Jerik's shattering into unstable insanity and launching into a death kill through one of his channels.

Jerik's emotions cracked wide open. Amazingly he curbed them away from his channels. "Kol Lenn, I've had enough of you. Aide to Hedrick or not, you are *not* on the same level as we of the Interworld Council. Your arrest may be valid, but your treatment of me is inexcusable. I assume you would have had your emotions flawlessly under control if you had been treated as I have been?"

The proximate continued to stand taut, his expression belying a sudden realization. His emotions were violently active, yet he was thinking clearly. Though furious at the aide, Jerik did not have to thrust at him with killing force, which seemed to be what Kol Lenn wanted him to do! The man had been goading him on! When he realized how to handle the situation, the proximate's intense rage died down. He relaxed against the guard's kinesis.

"Hedrick, your aide placed me under arrest for reasons that I feel are unwarranted. I trust you, as well as the rest of the Council, have read Adia's report."

"Yes," said Hedrick, eyeing Jerik carefully.

"Very well. I take it Kol Lenn pointed out only those sections which stated my apparent negative actions."

"Yes."

"Did your aide also wish to arrest me for completing our mission successfully with minimum casualties? Or does he wish to arrest me for murder because a few of my crew died in the line of duty on the last trip out of the warp? Does he know what the exact conditions were to ride the time warp? Has either Adia or I given him, as well as this Council, full informational transfer telepathy on the mission? Does he wish to arrest me because I knew Sael was needed with us? We would never have accomplished our mission had not that young man been on board."

"Guard, release Jerik," Hedrick said.

Jerik moved his arms and legs. His muscles were knotted from the tension that held him.

"Sir, I hardly think . . ." began Kol Lenn.

"Silence!" snapped Hedrick, rising and glaring at his aide with such ferocity that even Jerik paused in rubbing his sore arms.

Hedrick continued in the same tone. "Kol Lenn. I agreed, however reluctantly, to let you place my proximate under minor and temporary custody when you initially gave me your reasons from Adia's reports, pending a proper hearing—not a full-fledged trial!" He walked around the great hexagonal table to where his aide stood. "I said *minor* custody! That does not mean placing this man, whom I've had no grievance against, in a detainment cell and treating him like common scum!"

Hedrick paused, then added, "I think I've been listening to too much of your advice, Kol Lenn. You almost had me believing that my proximate was a criminal. I should have ignored you when you persuaded me to discount Sael's importance to the mission."

"Wait a moment," Jerik interrupted, walking over to Hedrick and the aide. His eyes narrowed. "Hedrick, when did Kol Lenn discuss Sael's coming with me?"

"While you were gone from your mansion, off in the Tieke Wildwoods."

Jerik's look pierced the aide. "Tell me, Kol Lenn, how did you know of my plan before I had a chance to tell Hedrick?"

"I am a penetration telepathist. It is my duty to bring up such matters to the first councillor," Kol Lenn said stiffly.

"I am aware of your duties," Jerik snapped. "Do they also include assassination attempts?"

The council members gasped with horror. The proximate advanced toward the aide and towered over him. "There are very few who know how to reach a council member mentally, even fewer who have penetration telepathy capable of extending past a councillor's blocks."

"You are accusing me?" Kol Lenn shouted over the commotion.

"Not only am I accusing you, but I now have proof you were the one. I never mentioned having Sael on board until I discussed it with Hedrick in my sitting chamber . . . except to Sael, of course. The brief thought flow that Sael received in his flash was well concealed, but not well enough, Kol Lenn. I couldn't place it at the time, but now I realize it matches yours.

"And shall I also mention your connection with the disaster Lym almost suffered? I found that out from the reports I saw in the far future. Persuaded by your advice, Hedrick chose someone not fully capable of handling the job of proximate after my disappearance. Hedrick died before he could train the man properly. As aide to the new first councillor you took over that training and neatly turned him away from the Plan: WORLDS IN UNISON THROUGH JUSTICE AND WISDOM. Disrupted, the Council system ground away until it developed into the chaos we saw."

"That is outrageous!" sputtered Kol Lenn. "Insane! You have no real proof!"

"Don't I?" Jerik said dangerously. "I have perfect recall of the reports I saw as well as Sael's flash of the attempt on our lives. The thought flow is identical to yours. I'd have Sael verify it himself, but he's in surgery right now. However, that's not necessary. The Council can judge its validity. I can't hide the truth from it. How about you, Kol Lenn?"

Without another word, the proximate opened his mind and allowed all present to examine the recall and the duplicate of Sael's flash with the vague wisp of thought flow permeating it. There was no doubt.

"Guilty of high treason and the assassination attempts!" Hedrick verified.

About to protest, Kol Lenn became aware of thirty-five councillors riveting their attention on him. It was too much. His emotions shattered. Unable to curb them, Kol Lenn launched into his only channel, blinded by hate.

Jerik knew the aide had a devastating reach with his channel. The proximate felt a crushing pressure in his mind but was prepared for it. Whipping into his own penetration channel, Jerik smashed against the attack and saw it was directed at the first councillor as well as himself. The two councilmen joined and blocked the aide's force, thrusting it back at him with sufficient power to knock Kol Lenn unconscious.

The elderly first councillor walked slowly to the hexagonal table and leaned heavily on it. Jerik motioned to the guard, who transported out of the room the unconscious aide. Then the proximate went to Hedrick and laid a hand on the first councillor's shoulder. Hedrick turned toward him. Jerik let his hand drop and quietly faced the man.

Hedrick's voice was steady, belying his exhaustion from the attack. "I am an old and foolish man to let an aide sway my judgment, especially when it comes to you, Jerik. Even more foolish not to detect his subtle treachery. He kept everything seemingly legal. That's why I listened to his advice about Sael. Originally I was considering allowing the young man on board. Undisciplined or not, his abilities were needed, and I am grateful that he made it on the mission. He will pull through surgery without disorientation problems, won't he?"

"Yes." Jerik vowed to make sure of it himself if he had to.

"Good. Then I think it high time to make a statement I should have made instead of taking Kol Lenn as my top aide. I have begun to make unwise decisions. I should have been able to detect Kol Lenn's treasonous qualities.

"None of us saw through him," Jerik interrupted.

"He wasn't your aide. You would have, had you chosen him. And you will detect any such treachery in the future. Because I am resigning."

Hedrick's slow walk back to his chair was the only sound in the meeting chamber. Jerik stared at him.

Hedrick sat and looked up at his proximate from across the wide room. "This world desperately needs someone to lead the people in the right direction. I am old and failing in my responsibility. You've got more than enough ability to lead your people. And don't think I didn't notice the way you curbed your emotions away from your channels today. Whatever you learned in the future, you carried back into the present. I don't doubt you'll be instituting special programs to teach our unstable population how to handle their emotions so we can have a sane world, a sane future for Galapix. You know in what direction to go. I need someone who can guide our people now. You're still young. You've got all the time you need. Use it with the wisdom and knowledge I know you have acquired in the past fourteen days."

A smile slowly spread out over Jerik's face. "Yes, sir!"

"One other thing," the first councillor continued, "it's going to take me about ten months to wrap everything up and get you completely prepared. Of course, with my departure, you'll be minus one member. My recommendations are for someone young and interested, with a full knowledge of space and a wide range of abilities, who still has access to his emotions and, most of all, who is willing to hold a Council position for life. Do any members dissent? No? Good! I think the present mission has proved him worthy."

Exactly ten months and fifteen days later First Councillor Hedrick resigned. During the resignation ceremony he conferred on Jerik the title of First Councillor of the Interworld Council. There was one other addition: Sael, bursting with pride, as the trained and new member of the Interworld Council was presented to the people by First Councillor Jerik.